About *Faraway Home,*

'The main characters are appealing, and the setting is intriguing in this
well-researched novel ... The real strength of the book, however,
lies in its realistic portrayal of Karl's feelings and of the
friendships he makes in his new surroundings.'
Booklist, magazine of the American Library Association

'History, written with the gripping reality of fiction. It is a story which,
like Anne Frank's diary, brings home to us all the horrific misery
inflicted by the Nazis – and the need to ensure that we never allow it
to happen again.' Lord Janner, QC, Holocaust Educational Trust

'The pathos, suffering and bravery are overwhelming. But for me, it is
Taylor's skill in building three-dimensional characters which makes
this book so outstanding. This is a story which stays with the reader,
long after the final page has been turned.' *Children's Books in Ireland*

'a remarkable blend of fiction and historical fact, which also reveals
a relatively unknown facet of World War Two'
Pauline Devine, *The Irish Times*

AWARDS FOR FARAWAY HOME

Winner, Irish Bisto Book of the Year Award
BBC Blue Peter Award
Included by the Association of Jewish Libraries in
'Best of the Bunch: Notable books of Jewish Interest'

MARILYN TAYLOR Born and educated in England, Marilyn has an economics degree from London University. A 'war-baby', she grew up in the shadow of the Holocaust in London in a family involved both in Jewish life and in local and national politics.

In Dublin, married with three children, she worked as a school librarian and later as college librarian in the Jesuit Library.

It was from the perspective of her Irish-Jewish experience that she began writing first for reluctant teenage readers, and more recently carefully researched historical fiction, engaging her young readers in readable stories, in particular on the themes of refugees, racism and diversity.

Long involved in the Irish-Jewish community, she recently co-edited a non-fiction book of photographs and vignettes on the history of Jewish Dublin.

Marilyn has visited numerous schools, libraries and arts festivals in Ireland, both North and South, in Britain, and in New York, speaking to young readers, teachers, librarians and parents. Her other novel in this genre is *Faraway Home*.

17 Martin Street

MARILYN TAYLOR

THE O'BRIEN PRESS
DUBLIN

First published 2008 by The O'Brien Press Ltd,
12 Terenure Road East, Rathgar, Dublin 6, Ireland.
Tel: +353 1 4923333; Fax: +353 1 4922777
E-mail: books@obrien.ie
Website: www.obrien.ie

ISBN 978-1-84717-125-2

British Library Cataloguing-in-publication Data
Taylor, Marilyn, 1940-
17 Martin Street
1. Neighbors - Juvenile fiction 2. Refugees - Juvenile fiction 3. Dublin (Ireland) -
Social life and customs - 20th century - Juvenile fiction 4. Children's stories
I. Title II. Seventeen Martin Street
823.9'14[J]

1 2 3 4 5 6 7 8 9 10
08 09 10 11 12 13 14 15

The O'Brien Press receives
assistance from

arts
council
chomhairle
ealaíon

Printed and bound in the UK by CPI Group

DEDICATION

For Hannah, Naomi, Dana, Samuel, Ariella,
Matan and Elinoa, and their parents,
to remind them – some time in the future –
of their Irish roots

ACKNOWLEDGEMENTS

All the people and institutions below gave me valued help with many aspects of this book.

I am especially grateful to my husband, Mervyn Taylor, without whose patient encouragement and support, and also factual knowledge and memories of his Dublin childhood, this book would probably not have been completed.

I would like to thank all at The O'Brien Press, and in particular my editor, Íde ní Laoghaire, whose tireless and enthusiastic help with the book over a long period, coupled with her kindness and consideration, are deeply appreciated.

My thanks to Renee Brompton, the Misses Cunningham (Greenville Terrace), David Elliott, Anne Kinsella, Donal McCay, Jacqueline and Willie Stein, Anita Weir, Marlene Wynn, Aubrey Yodaiken.

I also thank the Holocaust Educational Trust of Ireland (www.holocausteducationaltrustireland.org), the Irish Jewish Museum, Dublin City Libraries and South Dublin Libraries, especially Dolphin's Barn, Pearse Street, Rathmines and Ballyroan. I would like to thank librarian Hazel Foster and the staff of Terenure Library, Dublin, for their assistance and co-operation with my numerous research requests both for this book and over many years.

I should like to thank Colman Pearce for permission to include 'Growing up in Little Jerusalem', which originally appeared in *Jewish Dublin, Portraits of Life by the Liffey*, by Asher Benson.

If I am not for myself, who will be for me?

If I am for myself alone, what am I?

And if not now, when?

The Jewish Talmud

No man is an island,

Entire of itself.

Each is a piece of the continent

A part of the main

And therefore send not to know

For whom the bell tolls,

It tolls for thee.

John Donne, 'Meditation'

CONTENTS

Prologue

Extracts from Renata's Diary 1938-39
translated from the German

Berlin, Germany: December 1938

Early on these grey winter mornings I get up as soon as I wake, listening to a bird singing in the leafless tree in the garden. Then I creep down to the kitchen and sit beside the warm stove to write my diary. It helps me to try and make sense of all that's happening here in my home city where we've always lived.

My older brother, Walter, will be eighteen soon, but we won't be able to celebrate his birthday like we used to as things are too hard now. Mutti says Walter's 'a bit of a dreamer'. He always has a pencil in his pocket and draws our portraits – and they're really good. He gets my corn-coloured hair and green eyes just right. He wants to go to art school, but under the Nazis, Jews like us can't attend schools and colleges with everyone else like we used to, only Jewish schools.

My sister Ella is pretty and she loves dancing, but she's a bit spoilt because she's the youngest. She wants to go everywhere with me, which can be a nuisance. Though I'm fifteen, my parents still treat me like a child. They don't realise how quickly you grow up if you're a Jewish girl living in Nazi Germany.

These are not good times. Rumours are spreading of bad things happening to Jews and others, round-ups and prison camps – no one wants to believe them.

My best friend Dina and I often talk about boys and clothes and what we're going to do when we grow up. I want to be a doctor like Papa and she wants to marry and have six children, and be a famous actress too! But I'm afraid we're living in a dream world while the real world around us is growing darker and more threatening.

Papa explained that the Nazis, led by Adolf Hitler, are powerful and ruthless. They're using Jews as scapegoats for Germany's problems, taking away all we have.

Already we must hand in valuables. My aunt's flat was ransacked by the Nazi secret police, the Gestapo, and, because they found my great-grandmother's box of tiny, blackened silver coffee spoons, they took my aunt and uncle away – no one knows where.

My parents queue for hours every day with hundreds of others trying to get visas to leave. You need to have a job in another country, and that's very hard to get. Papa is from Poland, so we may go to Warsaw where we used to spend holidays with my grandparents. But yesterday he came home with a flash of hope in his eyes. He'd heard from a friend, Dr Lowy, about a small factory run by his Austrian cousin, Emil Hirsch, in a country called Ireland.

It's very far away, but Dr Lowy is trying to get jobs there for himself and Papa, though neither ever worked in a factory. Maybe we can all escape from Berlin, the city where we were happy – till the Nazis came, and the horror began.

Berlin, January 1939

Today there are deep snowdrifts. In the old days we used to go sledding and tobogganing, but now we're not allowed.

Things are getting worse, and Mutti has grown thin. Today Walter came home badly bruised. Seeing the yellow star that Jews have to wear on his jacket, Nazi Stormtroopers kicked and beat him when he refused to jump into the gutter to get out of their way. No one came to his aid. Battered and angry, he went straight to the Jewish Community Office to ask about ships to Palestine, the ancient country where Jews, young and old, are travelling to work the desert land.

Papa said Walter wasn't cut out to be a farmer, and when I reminded him about his dream of being an artist, he said he could work by day and study art at night. 'I refuse to be treated as an *untermensch* – I'm not sub-human,' he said heatedly, unlike his usual gentle manner. 'You should all come. Germany is a hell for us now.'

But Papa said he was expecting a visa for Ireland, and he would send for us from there. 'The British are in charge in Palestine and Jews can't get in there now,' he warned Walter. 'You could end up in a detention camp–'

'Couldn't be worse than the prison camps here,' Walter broke in.

Mutti wept, but a week later, with borrowed fare money and with our prayers and kisses, Walter departed, leaving us all desolate, like a tree with a branch cut off.

Berlin, March 1939

I miss Walter, my big brother who taught me to ride a bike and to skate, and always protected me. Ella keeps asking where he is now, but we've heard nothing.

People are disappearing – whole families – and we don't know if they've escaped from the Nazis or been sent to prison camps. Dina went without saying goodbye; her house is shuttered up and there are new people, Nazis, living there. Mutti heard Dina had escaped to Britain on a Kindertransport with other Jewish children. Our names are on the list, but thousands are trying to get out.

Then one day Papa came home with Dr Lowy, waving precious visas for them to work in Ireland.

As they drank tea, I asked, 'Where is Ireland?'

'It's near Britain – a small, beautiful island,' said Dr Lowy. 'It's lush and green because it rains a lot.'

'And it's not ruled by Nazis!' Papa picked up Ella and whirled her around.

'Still, they don't welcome refugees,' put in Dr Lowy. 'They allowed in a few people, including Emil, who's from Vienna, to set up factories employing local people.' He sighed. 'But hardly anyone gets in now, even if they're desperate.'

'Can we go tomorrow?' asked Ella.

But the visas were only for Papa and Dr Lowy.

'I'll find a way to get you all out of the clutches of the Nazis,' Papa told us, 'to safety in Ireland.'

I just hope he does.

Berlin, April 1939

It's so lonely without Papa. It's dangerous to go out and we miss our friends. Now I'm the eldest and I try to help Mutti and keep Ella cheerful. Although spring has come and the cherry trees are in bloom, our house feels empty and sad. As well as taking everything from us, the Nazis are breaking up our family. Who will be next to leave?

Papa has rented a room somewhere in Ireland. Mr Hirsch, the manager, helped him write to the Immigration Department in Dublin to get us entry papers. But though Papa has a job there, he still can't get permission to bring us over.

Our shoes are in holes. Ella cheered up when we went shopping, though we can only afford second-hand shoes, and anyway most shops won't sell to Jews. Ella complained that the wooden clogs we had to buy are very clumsy. 'I can't even skip in them.' She showed us and she was right.

As we returned, our neighbour rushed out. 'A black car full of SS men arrived after you left,' she told us fearfully. We all knew these were the Nazi officers in leather coats and polished boots. They had rapped on our door. 'They'll come back,' she whispered. 'You must all leave.'

We were terrified, but Mama told us to pack warm clothes quickly. Tonight we will take the train for Warsaw where Papa's family will take us in.

On the train – no time to write more –

Warsaw, Poland, August 1939
We're in a small house with my grandparents, uncle, two aunts and our cousins. Warsaw is a fine city, though we've heard there are people here too who hate Jews.

But Christian friends of Papa, Casimir and Berta Pavlak, have helped us with money and food. They're angry at what's happening in Germany to Jews, and also to others, even Christians, and they pray the Nazis don't invade Poland. So do we.

Until Mutti can get a sewing machine she helps my aunts do other people's washing by hand on a wooden board. It's very hard work, and sweaty too – I hope I don't have to do it. The whole house smells of soap-suds and damp clothes.

We're all homesick for Berlin as it was before the Nazis. I miss Dina and my other friends and the fun we all used to have. Today Papa sent us some money, and writes that he has a plan to get a temporary Irish visa for me. But only for me.

When I heard this I burst into tears. How can I travel alone to a faraway land, without Mutti and Ella? When would I see them again?

Uncle said, 'It's hard to be uprooted again, Renata, but you must go.' He explained that if the Nazis invaded Poland they would force all Jews into a kind of ghetto, where thousands would live crowded together in hunger, misery and disease. We shivered.

'If Papa gets you a visa,' Uncle added, 'maybe he'll get your mother and Ella out later.'

'And then,' Mutti said, trying to smile, 'we'll be together in Ireland.' No one said: Except Walter.

So now I know – the next one in my family to leave will be me!

1

The Rescue

Dublin, Ireland, Winter 1940

'Ben, did'ya hear? The canal's frozen over.'

Ben Byrne looked up from his bowl of porridge. Beside him his brother, Sean, was wolfing down slices of fried bread as fast as Granny could tip them, sizzling, out of the heavy frying pan and on to his plate.

'It's great gas,' Sean went on. 'Everyone's sliding on the ice, even kicking a football around on it.' Between mouthfuls he said to Ben, 'You could go down after school and have a game with Smiler and the others.'

Sean, three years Ben's senior, strong and thickset with a loud voice, spoke in the condescending tone he'd acquired since he and some of his pals had become official messengers helping with Air Raid Protection in the Emergency. They whizzed around Dublin on their bikes, sporting ARP armbands and gas masks slung in a box over the handlebars, collecting buckets and hoses for fire practice. There'd been no attacks or fires so far, but that didn't seem to weaken their enthusiasm or sense of importance.

'Don't you be playing games on the ice, Ben,' Granny put in quickly. 'It's treacherous. We've enough trouble in the family as it is.' She turned to Sean. 'You should know better, a big lad of fifteen, working and all–'

But Sean, muttering 'late for work', grabbed his packet of jam sandwiches, hauled his bike outside and dashed off to his new delivery job at the White Heather laundry.

* * *

Early that morning fresh snow had fallen and when Ben stepped into the white street he was aware of a strange, muffled hush.

But later, coming home from school, his hands so stiff with cold that he could barely grip the strap around his school books, the snow in Synge Street had been stirred into a grey, lumpy mush by people and horses and the few cars that were still around these days.

Ben peeled off from the other boys, who were calling to the sweet shop on the corner of St Kevin's Road to get sticks of liquorice or maybe even a hard-to-find KitKat bar. But though Sean was working now, Ben knew his Mam's sickness was costing the family, and he didn't even have a penny, let alone twopence for a KitKat.

The canal lay at the end of Martin Street in Portobello, where the Byrne family – Mam and Dad, Granny, Sean and Ben – had moved a year earlier from a teeming tenement in New Street where the boys had grown up.

Ben still hadn't got used to the green peace of the

canal bank. The grass, in summer soft and lush, was now stiff and frosty, scraping Ben's bare knees as he squatted down. Instead of the procession of low barges carrying turf sliding slowly past, there was now a sheet of greyish-white ice, shining in the distance like a mass of tiny diamonds. There was no sign of a football game, but further down children were sliding, falling and shrieking on their new icy playground.

Idly, Ben was wondering where all the ducks went when their watery home froze, when there was a sudden movement beside him. A man appeared, flung a bulging sack into the canal, and made off.

The ice cracked and the sack sank into the murky water. Ben jumped to his feet as it surfaced again. It moved strangely, with high-pitched squeaks issuing from it.

Seconds later a girl came from nowhere, running like a deer towards Ben, her eyes on the sack. It was now almost submerged in the dark circle that had opened up in the ice.

Reaching the edge of the bank the girl squatted down and began to unlace her boots. 'Quick,' she said urgently to Ben, 'there's something alive in that sack.'

'It isn't safe,' he told her, uncertain what to do. 'We should get help.'

'There's no time,' she snapped.

Granny's words that morning flashed across Ben's

mind. Surely it wasn't worth taking a risk on the ice? But he turned and saw the girl's face clearly – a mop of dark curly hair and angry, blazing eyes commanding him to help. He picked up a fallen branch from the bank.

'I'll slide over and try to fish it out,' he said, with a bravado he didn't really feel. 'You hang on to me in case the ice gives way.' He took off his glasses and put them in his pocket.

Gingerly, he lay face down on the ice, which was as rigid as iron yet fragile as eggshells beneath him. The cold burned his skin as he inched towards the sack, now almost completely underwater and hardly moving. Cautiously sliding closer, he reached out with the stick, trying unsuccessfully to lever the bundle up out of the jagged hole.

Fear stopped him short. Even if he reached the sack, how was he going to get it – and himself – back to the bank?

There was a touch on his leg. Turning his head, his face stinging from ice-burn, he realised the girl had tied something to his ankle.

'It's all right,' she called. 'I'll pull you back. Be careful not to crack the ice.'

Encouraged, he slid a little further along. Using the stick and all his strength, he managed to raise the sodden sack out of the water.

Exhausted, he lay spread-eagled, his numb fingers clutching a corner of the sack, now ominously still and silent.

There were a few tugs on his ankle as the girl attempted unsuccessfully to pull him in. Raising his head he looked back. Without his glasses everything was a blur. He was a prisoner, almost unable to move, his strength waning.

After what seemed like an age he felt another, stronger tug, and found himself slowly and painfully gliding back to the bank. Then, still grasping the sack, he was back on the grass. With an effort he rolled over and saw the heavy winter sky leaning down over him.

Shakily he sat up and put on his glasses, his face and body chilled yet burning, and his legs sore and scratched. He and the passer-by who'd helped pull him in watched as the girl opened the sack and scooped out three puppies. They all inspected the tiny, pathetic creatures – two chocolate brown splotched with white, wriggling, the third stiff and silent.

'Looks like *he's* a goner,' said the man who had helped.

Gazing down at the little creatures with anger and pity, the girl muttered, 'How could anyone do such a wicked thing?'

'They probably couldn't afford to feed them. Times are

hard,' said the man. 'Stay off that ice, now.' And he went away.

'It's so cruel.' She clutched the puppies to her, and to his embarrassment Ben saw a tear trickle down her cheek.

'At least we saved two,' he muttered awkwardly.

'I must get them to my uncle's to feed them,' she said. 'He lives near here.' And without a word of thanks or farewell, she hastened off, the puppies in her arms.

Ben was left sore, uncomfortable and puzzled. Unusually, he had done something that required courage – mostly thanks to that girl. And now she'd just gone.

Back at home, he didn't dare tell his dad about the incident. He told Granny he'd slipped, wincing as she dabbed his sore legs with lint soaked in brown iodine.

But in the weeks ahead he often replayed the scene in his mind, wondering if he'd ever find out the fate of the puppies, or who that furious, headstrong girl was.

2

New Neighbours

A few weeks later Ben, seated on the edge of his iron bed in the chilly upstairs bedroom of Number 19 Martin Street, was watching out for the glimmer man.

Further down the street between the rows of terraced houses, packed tight as teeth, a football game was in progress. The shouts of his brother Sean and Ben's friend Eamon – known as Smiler on account of his cheerful nature – echoed enticingly up from the street. But he was stuck here for another half-hour, while downstairs in the kitchen Granny hurried to make tea before Dad left for the early-evening shift with the Local Defence Force, the LDF.

Ben could lean out and roar through the window to Smiler, or maybe Sean, to come and take a turn on the watch. But in the next room their mother lay sick, and if he woke her, he'd be murdered.

Ben had never actually seen the glimmer man – a uniformed inspector from the Gas Company who cycled around the streets of Dublin on an orange bicycle. If he discovered anyone evading gas rationing by lighting the tiny whiff left in the pipes when the gas was officially turned off, then the Gas Company might fine them, or even cut off their gas altogether so they couldn't cook anything except over a smoky fire. 'And then,' as Granny said, 'how would we feed a family with two hungry boys?'

So it was Ben's task to watch out and warn Granny and the neighbours. Ben pictured the official striding into the kitchen and putting his hand on the gas ring to check if it was warm – proof that Granny had been cooking on the 'glimmer'. He imagined Granny in tears, his dad raging that he'd have no hot tea before he left, his mam up in bed listening anxiously to the commotion below. He sighed – better forget about football and concentrate on his lookout job.

He was almost nodding off with boredom when from the far end of the street he heard a distant grinding rumble, too noisy to be the glimmer man's bike. Slowly, an odd procession came into view: a woman in a drab woollen dress and headscarf, carrying a bundle of blankets. Behind her, hunched with the effort of pushing a laden handcart, was a bearded man in a long overcoat and soft felt hat, and two girls, the younger about Ben's age.

As the cart ground to a halt below, the man straightened up, mopping his forehead with a handkerchief. Approaching the house next door to Ben's, empty since old Granny Murphy had gone to live with her daughter, he peered at the number, took out a key and unlocked the front door.

New neighbours at last! Pity there was no sign of a boy his own age who might become a friend, joining in the football or playing marbles or conkers or swapping cigarette cards. When Ben had first come to live in Martin Street only a year ago, some local boys had called out mockingly, 'Specky Four-eyes!' on account of his glasses. Smiler, a bit younger than Ben, was his only real friend here, and he still missed the pals he'd grown up with in New Street.

Below, the woman entered Number 17, cradling the bundle which Ben could now see was a baby wrapped in blankets. The others all seized parcels and boxes, and began to carry them inside.

Ben leant perilously out of the window to watch. Should he go down and offer to help? The older girl spotted him and said something to the younger one. Staggering under the weight of a heavy box, the younger girl followed her sister's glance, squinting up into the wintry sun; then, frowning, she tossed her mass of curly hair and bent down.

Ben wiped his smeary glasses and had another look. There was something familiar about her. And then she opened the box and let out a frisky brown and white puppy, which darted in and out of everyone's legs, yapping furiously.

Ben nearly fell out of the window. It was her, *that* girl!

He recognised now the unruly hair and the thick eye-brows drawn together in a frown. And the puppy must be one he himself had helped to rescue. What had happened to the other? And why was that girl so cross? Didn't she recognise him? As questions buzzed in his mind the family below speedily humped in all the boxes and furniture and disappeared inside the house.

* * *

'Ben, the gas is on!' The welcome shout floated up from downstairs. 'Come and get your tea.'

From Mam's room, beside his and Sean's, there was no sound. Trying to stop his boots from clattering on the bare wooden stairs, he ran down.

At the bottom he cannoned into Sean, dashing in from the street. 'You missed a great game,' he told Ben. Ben grunted. Trust Sean to add salt to the wound.

They sat at the table opposite their dad, hidden behind the *Evening Mail,* and began to eat the sausages and baked beans dished out by Granny.

'That old damp turf,' she grumbled as their eyes watered from the acrid smoke billowing out from the grate. 'There's barely any heat out of it. God be with the days when we had coal.'

'It's the war,' grunted Dad, getting up to grab his tin hat and bicycle clips from a hook on the door.

The war ... Ben thought back to the golden September day when a newsboy had appeared in the street shouting, 'Stop press – read all about it!' Mam had given Sean a penny and he'd sped back with the *Evening Herald,* its stark headline in huge black letters: WAR DECLARED.

In the hall of the tenement house a neighbour who'd fought with British troops in the last war had declared, 'Britain'll trounce Hitler and the Nazis.'

But the old man from upstairs grunted: 'Those Nazis in Germany know how to run a country. If they came here we'd get real independence – all thirty-two counties.'

'The Nazis are *against* independence for anyone,' Mam said sharply. 'They want to rule the world, and they hate Jews and gypsies and black people and anyone that's different from them. *And* trade unions that stand up for decent working people like us.'

Later, Mam had still been furious. 'Your Uncle Matt fought against that evil crowd already in Spain,' she'd reminded Ben and Sean. 'Some people never learn.'

* * *

In the kitchen Granny poked at the weak fire. 'It says in the papers there's no war here,' she muttered to Dad, 'only an Emergency.'

'Whatever it's called, at least we're not in it,' said Dad shortly.

'Still, flour and tea are scarce,' grumbled Granny. 'No coal or petrol. And it's a hard winter.'

'Sure, how could *you* feel the cold, Granny,' teased Sean, 'with all you have on?'

'That's enough, Sean,' said Dad, as, like a hen with ruffled feathers, Granny indignantly smoothed down her clothes. Ben fought back a grin, thinking of Granny's ganseys, flannel petticoats, woollen combinations and thick black stockings that hung out to dry with the rest of the washing every Monday in the sooty back yard.

Then Dad's face became stern. 'Listen here to me, now,' he said heavily. 'There's new people moved in next door, and I don't want anyone getting too pally with them.'

Sean looked up from his tea. 'Why not?'

'They're foreigners,' Dad replied sharply. 'Jews.'

'But there's lots of Jewish families in Portobello,' said Granny. 'Sure, they even call it Little Jerusalem.'

'There's some living here in Martin Street – Joey and Mickser Woolfson play football with us,' put in Sean. 'Why–'

'Because I say so!' Ben jumped as Dad banged his fist on the table. 'I'm telling you, stay away from that house.' There was a silence. He went on, 'There's too many of these foreigners here. They're different from us, and there isn't work for us all. They should go back where they came from.'

Granny, tight-lipped, handed him his sandwiches. They all knew to keep quiet when Dad was in one of his angry moods, especially without Mam on hand to smooth him over.

Fixing on his bicycle clips he grunted, 'I'm late.' Then he added, his voice softening, 'I'll just look in on Marie.' They heard him tip-toe up the stairs.

While he was drying the dishes, Ben thought over what Dad had said. The other Jewish neighbours seemed to get on well with the people in the street, and, like Sean said, everyone played together. But his dad was so certain they didn't really belong here. And anyway, that girl hadn't appeared too friendly, even though he'd helped her rescue the puppies.

Dad trundled his bike through the kitchen and with relief they heard the front door slam. Through the lace-curtained parlour window Ben glimpsed him, in tin hat and green uniform, wobbling off down the road.

* * *

After his father had left, Ben climbed the stairs. From Mam's room came the familiar racking cough that the bottle from Mushatt's chemist hadn't cured. Ben tapped at the door.

Lying in the brass bed, a cream-coloured Aran shawl around her shoulders, she beckoned him in. Her long, auburn hair, once lustrous and wound into a loose knot secured with hairpins, now hung lank and dull. But her level green eyes still shone; and though holding a hand-kerchief to her mouth, she smiled the old smile.

'How're you, Benny love?' About to reach out to him, she drew back, mindful of the risk of infection. 'Did you get your tea?'

He nodded. 'Mam, there's new people next door' and he repeated Dad's comments.

She frowned. 'Ben, those people are just a different religion.'

'But Dad said—'

'Poor Dad has a lot on his mind, but he shouldn't bad-mouth them. Growing up down the country he never knew any Jews.' She struggled to heave herself up in the bed. 'But Granny and your uncle Matt and me – we grew up in Lennox Street and we were friends with all the Jewish neighbours.' She paused, and added hoarsely, 'They've always been at the wrong end of things, wher-ever they live.'

An image of the dark-haired girl shot into Ben's mind, 'Where'd they come from?'

'Mostly Eastern Europe. They had bad times there. Some of our own leaders – James Connolly and Michael Davitt – spoke of killings and persecution of Jews in Russia' – she broke off to cough – 'and now again in Nazi Germany.'

Uncle Matt, Mam's older brother, often talked about the war, especially since his son, Ben's cousin Paddy, had volunteered along with thousands of Irish men and women, to fight with the British forces. And from reading the papers to his uncle, whose sight was failing, Ben knew the Nazis were marching through Europe; they'd even conquered France, and their U-boats were sinking British ships in the Atlantic.

Still, none of this appeared to Ben to have much to do with Ireland or Martin Street or the new neighbours in Number 17. And whatever Mam said, Ben shrank from facing his dad's anger.

Although a bar of the hissing gas heater glowed in the fireplace, Mam shivered, drawing the shawl round her. 'I'd better rest now, pet.' She blew him a kiss, her frail white hand fluttering like a bird trying to fly.

As he left, longing for her to hug him like she used to, she murmured, 'Never forget, Benny, both our religions come from the same roots.'

* * *

Later, Ben walked home from a game of conkers at Smiler's house, his shiny brown champion in his pocket. He'd found it last autumn crunching through the russet chestnut leaves, extracted it from its prickly nest and baked it hard in the grate. Threaded on a string and swung against the others' conkers till one broke, his champion had survived. One more win, Ben exulted, and it would be a 'sixer' – a six-times winner.

As he hurried past the uncurtained window of Number 17 he glimpsed the new family sitting around a table on which two candles flickered in brass candlesticks. Beside the bearded man who'd pushed the cart was an older man, a black skullcap on his silver hair. Then the younger girl entered the room and placed two steaming bowls before them.

Recalling her scowl and his father's bitter words, he hurried past, pushing open his own front door, left on the latch while Granny was at her sodality meeting. As he climbed the stairs, he heard a low murmur from his mother's room as Uncle Matt paid his evening visit.

That night, after he'd said his prayers, Ben's thoughts lingered on the house next door, identical to his own, but, somehow, now different.

Still, despite Mam's kinder words, Dad had made it crystal clear that if Sean or Ben had anything to do with those people, including that disturbing girl, they'd be in trouble.

3

17 Martin Street

Earlier that afternoon in Number 17, Leon Golden leaned back in the one battered armchair they had, stroking his beard thoughtfully while around him twelve-year-old Hetty, her older sister Mabel and their mother, Sarah, scurried around unpacking boxes and parcels. In the midst of the flurry, the baby slept peacefully in a large wooden drawer that, lined with blankets, served as a crib. The puppy, named Mossy by Hetty because he'd been rescued from drowning like baby Moses in the Bible, lay curled up on the floor beside him.

'Does anyone know where my books are?' asked Leon vaguely.

Hetty, half-way up the steep stairs with a bundle of worn flannel sheets in her arms, stopped to ease the ache in her shoulders. Her winter vest and green woollen dress – a hated hand-me-down from her sister – stuck to her body, and her head throbbed.

They'd been up since dawn packing their belongings in the two cluttered rooms above the tailoring shop in Mary Street where their father worked sewing the button-holes into coats and jackets.

Together the family had heaved the handcart over the

slippery cobbles and setts down to the quays, across the greeny-grey waters of the Liffey at Capel Street bridge, skirted Dublin Castle, on through the fringes of the Liberties teeming with stalls and barrows, and finally across the South Circular Road – thronged and noisy with trams, horse-drawn carts and bikes – to Portobello.

'Get on with it, Hetty, there's loads more stuff to bring up.' Mabel, her round, cheerful face shining with sweat, squeezed past Hetty on the stairs. 'Did you see our room?'

Hetty followed her sister up into the back bedroom, with its sloping ceiling.

'Look,' exclaimed Mabel, pointing to the empty grate, 'our own fireplace! Though I suppose we'll only be allowed a fire if we're sick.'

'*Really* sick,' said Hetty.

In Mary Street the whole family had shared a bedroom divided only by a curtain, and there had been no yard. Hetty felt a thrill of pleasure at the prospect of a separate bedroom for herself and Mabel. Leaning out of the narrow window, they gazed out over the tiny concrete back yard with its outside toilet and coal bunker, to the startlingly close backs of a row of houses in the next street, Kingsland Parade.

A wail from downstairs announced that the baby was up. Mossy came lolloping up the stairs and whined outside their bedroom door.

'Girls,' called Ma. 'Come and sort the pots and pans while I feed the baby.'

'Lucky little Solly,' grumbled Mabel. 'What about us? I'm starving.'

'First I'm going to scrounge something for Mossy,' announced Hetty as they clattered downstairs. 'He's also a baby, you know.'

* * *

The baby and the puppy had been fed and most of the boxes unpacked before Ma handed out kichels – sweet homemade raisin cookies – and cups of 'shell cocoa', which Da always complained was dreadful as it was made from the husks and shells of the cocoa beans in-stead of the real thing. Everyone hated it but had to make do with it because of the war.

Hetty heard a hesitant tap on the front window, their grandfather's way of announcing his arrival. 'It's Zaida!' she cried, jumping up to let him in.

Zaida, in his heavy old greatcoat, a worn trilby hat on his strong silver hair, entered, carrying a bulging paper bag, his face creased with smiles.

'*Mazal tov*!' he said. 'Good luck and blessings in the new house!' They hugged him, and he pinched their cheeks affectionately, fishing in his coat pocket, always full of goodies. Handing Fry's chocolate cream bars to the girls and a bag of pungent-smelling pear drops to Ma, along with the bag of food, he said, 'Bobba sent something for your Friday night dinner.' He looked round. 'Where's little Solly?'

'He's asleep,' said Ma. 'Please thank Bobba for the meal.'

'Come and see over the house,' said Da.

When they returned Zaida sank down, wheezing, into the armchair as Da poured him a small whiskey, kept for the Sabbath. 'A fine house.'

'After Mary Street, it's a palace,' called Ma from the kitchen.

'How's Bobba's rheumatism?' asked Da.

'Well, she's able to give out to me about everything – the damp turf, no white flour.' Zaida's eyes twinkled. 'Even the cold weather's my fault!' He sipped the whiskey. 'Your Uncle Sam will be over later to see the new place,' he said to the girls. 'Eddie too.'

'How's Cousin Eddie getting on with his Barmitzvah studies?' asked Mabel, as she and Hetty hurried in and out of the kitchen, unpacking candlesticks and cutlery and setting the table.

'Eddie's smart, especially at Hebrew studies,' said Da approvingly. 'I'm sure he'll do well on the big day.'

'Still, nothing's easy for children with polio,' said Zaida. 'The disease does such damage to the body.'

'Well, at least now we're nearer, we can see him more often,' said Hetty, with rare warmth.

Mabel carried in Solly, who looked around curiously with big dark eyes, and smiled as Zaida made clucking noises. Ma, wiping her hands on her apron, hurried in from the kitchen and lit the two tall waxy candles, covering her face with her hands as she recited the Sabbath blessing. Da poured the sweet red wine into tiny cups and handed them around with chunks of *challah*, the plaited Sabbath bread, fragrant with poppy seeds, baked that morning by Bobba. Then the children were blessed and Zaida dropped a kiss on Solly's downy head.

'I'm starving,' Hetty murmured to Mabel as they carried in bowls of golden chicken soup swimming with noodles, the first two, as usual, for Zaida and Da.

Then there was chicken with roast potatoes, and Ma brought in an earthenware bowl, announcing, 'Bobba's special sweet carrot stew with dumplings!'

'Yummy!' said Mabel.

Just as they finished, Uncle Sam, their Da's brother, and his son, Eddie, arrived.

Glasses of tea were brought in, and Uncle Sam jigged Solly up and down on his knee. Hetty waited for the subject that always came up these days – the war.

'Did you hear about the air raids on London and Coventry?' asked Uncle Sam.

'Yes, we're lucky to be living here,' said Da, 'away from the real war.'

Uncle Sam lowered his voice. 'When the Nazis march in, first thing they do is round up the Jews.'

Hetty had heard this before. 'But why can't they get away?' she put in. 'To here, or other countries not in the war?'

They all looked at her in surprise, not used to her taking part in adult conversation. Da snapped, 'You're too young to understand these things, Hetty.'

But Uncle Sam explained patiently, 'The ones with foresight emigrated as soon as the Nazis came to power. A few even got work at a factory in the west of Ireland a couple of years ago.' He sighed. 'But now Jews need money and visas to get out; most countries, Ireland too, won't admit penniless refugees.'

'Please God the Nazis don't come here,' said Ma quietly.

Da frowned. 'Sarah, you'll frighten the children–'

'We're not such children,' snapped Hetty. 'If the Nazis come here, we'll be–'

'That's enough, Hetty,' shouted Da. 'Always answering back.' In the silence that followed, Ma pressed Solly close to her heart.

'Anyone heard the rumours about this German girl who's supposed to have escaped to Dublin?' enquired

Eddie. Hetty glanced at him. Trust Eddie to help her out. She smiled a rare smile at her favourite cousin.

'Nobody knows where she is,' said Uncle Sam. 'It may only be a rumour.'

Hetty interrupted him. 'Well, if it's true, and someone doesn't find her soon she'll be sent back. And what'll happen to her then?'

What could she do to help this girl, Hetty wondered, carrying out the dishes with Mabel. Instead of all this talk, surely they should be searching for any refugees who might have escaped to here and had nowhere to go? Hetty made a decision: *she* would keep her eyes and ears open.

Later, the washing-up done, Ma put Solly down on a blanket on the floor. He sat unsteadily, grabbing at his toes and tipping over as he tried to pull them up and stuff them in his mouth, making them all laugh.

'Come, Papa,' Uncle Sam said to Zaida. 'I'll walk you home.'

Zaida rose and turned to Ma. 'May the family live here in peace and good health.' Then, out of earshot of their father, busily unpacking prayer books, he murmured to her, 'I'll pray things will be better for you here, my dear.'

Hetty and Mabel, overhearing, exchanged glances. Zaida said to them quickly, 'Maybe one day you'll both get married from this house! We'll have such *nachas*, such pride and joy!'

Mabel looked bashful, but Hetty, hating this kind of talk, frowned.

Zaida reminded them, 'Don't be late for synagogue tomorrow.'

As they kissed their parents goodnight a short time later, Da said gently, as he did every night, 'Goodnight, children; God bless, happy dreams.' He patted Hetty's shoulder to show she was forgiven.

* * *

Hetty groaned inwardly as she hurried out, shivering, to the lavatory in the yard. If only they could miss the Sabbath service for once and have a lie-in in their new room. But Zaida, his eyes on the ladies' gallery in the synagogue, would notice their absence, and no one liked to upset him.

'I'm sure we're going to be happy here,' said Mabel dreamily as the girls undressed and washed quickly in a basin of cold water.

'It has to be better than Mary Street,' said Hetty, pulling her Locknit pyjamas on over her vest and jumping into the sagging bed.

'And to have our own room—'

'Even if it's freezing.' Hetty sat up in bed vigorously brushing her hair till it crackled and sparked.

Mabel was examining her face for pimples in the old,

spotted mirror. 'It'll be even more freezing downstairs tomorrow,' she told Hetty. 'Pity we've no *Shabbos goy* to come and light the fire in the morning.'

Hetty made a face. It was sometimes a nuisance not being allowed to work on the Sabbath – even something as simple as flicking a switch or lighting the fire. 'Surely there's a child in the street who'd like to earn a penny?'

'Ma knocked next door,' replied Mabel. 'She said smoke was coming from the chimney but no one answered.'

'The house where that boy with specs was watching us?'

Mabel nodded. 'He was staring so hard I thought he was going to fall out the window.'

After a moment Hetty said casually: 'He looked a bit like the boy I told you about at the canal that day we rescued the puppies. He had specs too.'

'Surely he'd have recognised Mossy and come and asked about them?'

'If it *was* him, it shows he doesn't care about them,' persisted Hetty. 'I gave him a really dirty look.'

'It mightn't have been him,' retorted Mabel. 'You know you need specs yourself.' She added patronisingly, 'When I start earning I'll buy them for you – they're only two shillings in Woolworth's.'

Selecting several thin, bendy pipe-cleaners from a bag she began curling her fair hair expertly round each one, securing it with a hairpin. 'Maybe he was just shy.'

Looking like a porcupine, she climbed into bed beside her sister. 'You're always so angry, Hetty.' Snuggling under the threadbare blankets she went on, 'Anyway, there's other families around.' Giggling, she went on, 'Ma said we might meet some nice, suitable boys tomorrow in Greenville Hall Synagogue.'

'I don't want to meet any boys, especially suitable ones,' Hetty said, yawning. 'There's more important things to think about, like the war, and what's happening to Jews in Europe–'

It was Mabel's turn to yawn. 'Yes, it's awful. But what can *we* do?' She lay down carefully, keeping her head rigid on the pillow. 'I mean, it's all so far away.'

'Still, there might be refugees here in Dublin,' insisted Hetty, 'in hiding, like that girl Eddie was talking about.'

No answer from Mabel except a snore. Hetty tried to switch her thoughts away from war and refugees. Through the thin wall she could hear the baby whimpering and a low murmur from her parents. At least they weren't arguing. In Mary Street there'd been rows, mainly over Da gambling his wages on the horses.

Maybe that would change here in Martin Street, like Zaida said. As long as they could pay the rent every week all would be fine. Her last thought as she drifted off to sleep, though, was of that nosy boy peering down at them from the upstairs window. Was he the boy from the canal?

4

The Broken Window

'Come on, Ben, forget the glimmer man, Billy's doing a message in Clanbrassil Street and then we're going to try out the football he got from his uncle.' It was a holy day, school was closed, and Smiler was at the door, with his neighbour Billy Flynn. Ben glanced at Granny, who said encouragingly: 'Go on with you, Ben. It's time you got out. Don't forget your scarf.' She gave them each a freshly baked jam tart and off they went, picking up Maurice Woolfson – known to everyone as Mickser – further along the street.

The boys walked up the South Circular Road, busy with traffic, and into bustling Lower Clanbrassil Street, lined with kosher bakeries and butchers' shops, along with watchmakers, grocers, drapers and wine-sellers. Billy and Smiler couldn't resist bouncing and kicking the new ball all the way up the noisy street, through a heaving mass of people chatting, the older ones in Yiddish; tempting smells of pickled cucumbers, spices and hot bread wafted from all sides.

Billy collected his father's boots which had been repaired at Atkins, and then Mickser darted into Weinrock's bakery and emerged, grinning, with three bagels, marked down because they were yesterday's. Ben munched the delicious bagel – he loved these round bread rolls with the hole in the middle and crispy onions and poppy seed on top. Turning into Lombard Street they started an impromptu game with the new ball and were soon joined by local children. After the ball just missed a passing cyclist, a woman told them they shouldn't be playing there. Ben was uneasy, but as soon as she'd passed, the game continued.

Not wanting to be a spoilsport, Ben said nothing. Caught up in the momentum of the game, he received one of Billy's famous headers and gave an almighty kick which Mickser, running, tripped and missed. As they watched in horror, the ball zoomed on to hit a white-haired old man who'd just emerged from Rubenstein's butcher's shop on the corner, with a newspaper-wrapped parcel under his arm. Then, bouncing hard off him, knocking him off balance, the ball hit the plate-glass shop window, smashing it to smithereens.

'Run!' shouted Billy, and they all sprinted off down Lombard Street. But Ben had never been a fast runner, and after a couple of minutes, breathless and terrified, his glasses slipping down his nose, he felt a heavy hand on his shoulder. Just my luck, he thought miserably as the Guard marched him back to the shop, crunching over innumerable shards of glass which covered the path. And there stood the old man, dazed but upright, still clutching his parcel.

Only then did Ben realise who it was – the old man he'd spied that night through the window of the house next door.

* * *

People crowded around and someone brought a chair for the old man, who seemed as breathless as Ben.

'Now, young fella,' grunted the Guard, 'look what you're after doing!'

Ben looked around hopelessly for the others. Eyes on the ground, he stammered, 'S-s-sorry … I, er, we … d-didn't–'

A ruddy-faced man in a blood-stained apron appeared from the shop and said angrily: 'You'll have to pay for this! And there's this poor man as well–'

'It wasn't just me,' muttered Ben. But he knew the offending kick had been his.

Then the old man spoke up. 'Just a minute, young man.'

Ben forced himself to look up, and was taken aback to see the man wasn't consumed with rage as he had expected. In fact, he was saying mildly, in a strange, guttural accent: 'You needn't look so terrified. I'm not hurt. I played football myself when I was a boy in our *shtetl*, our village in Lithuania. I know it can get out of hand.' And he smiled a sweet, kindly smile, showing broken teeth. 'Where do you live?'

'Martin Street,' stuttered Ben, wondering would the old man arrive at his house to complain to his father.

The Guard, wanting to be off, butted in. 'He'll have to pay.' The butcher nodded vigorous agreement.

'I ... haven't any money,' Ben mumbled to the old man. 'It's hard to get jobs ...' Perhaps he could ask Uncle Matt, and maybe the others would pay something? But if Dad heard about it ... He gulped down tears.

The old man stood up and said in a low voice to the butcher and the Guard: 'You can see the child has nothing. I will pay for the window.'

The Guard objected, 'Ah no, these young ones need to learn a lesson.'

'Of course,' said the old man. 'The children can each pay me five shillings towards it. I'll give this boy a weekly job so he can pay me back bit by bit.'

The crowd, realising there were no real casualties and no row, was beginning to drift away.

Ben felt a surge of relief. A job would be all right – but what kind of job would it be?

'It's all the same to me,' said the butcher. 'As long my window's replaced.' His wife was already sweeping the glass into a heap. Ben ineffectually tried to help.

'I have to go,' said the old man, holding up his parcel. 'My wife's waiting for this chicken.'

'Er, th-thank you,' murmured Ben, longing to get away from the whole mess.

'So you must come tomorrow morning, that's *Shabbos*, the Sabbath, and every Saturday to kindle the fire,' the man went on. 'Two pence a week.'

Two pence! Though he'd have to pay towards the window, there might be a bit left to get something for his mother.

'Where d'you live?' Ben ventured.

The man smiled. 'Oh, it's not for us. Our neighbour's daughter does that. It's for my son, Leon Golden, and his family. They live near you, at 17 Martin Street, and they need a *Shabbos goy*!'

5

The Shabbos Goy

Ben sped home from Clanbrassil Street. The only time he'd even come near trouble like this was 'boxing the fox' in the orchards in Rathmines and Rathgar. Even then, he'd always been the timid one, hanging back, admiring the courage of Sean and the others, but not really enjoying the apples they'd picked in case the Guards caught them.

In Martin Street he saw Smiler perched on the window-sill of his own house waiting for him. 'Sorry you got caught,' he said with a sheepish grin. 'I nearly did too.'

Hearing Ben's story he hastened inside and brought out two shiny half-crowns from his precious bike savings. 'My sister does that, lighting the fire and switching on lights for the people round the corner,' he said, 'and she only gets a penny and some sweets.' But, thought Ben, Smiler's sister didn't have Ben's dad to reckon with.

As Ben turned towards home, Smiler asked him, 'What's that they call that job?'

Ben lowered his voice and reeled off the explanation the old man had given. '*Shabbos* is what they call their Sabbath, and *goy* means a stranger – someone who isn't Jewish.'

'But *they're* the strangers, not us,' protested Smiler.

'Well, we're not Jews, are we? So I'm a *goy* to them and

so are all of us.' said Ben. 'And listen, you're not to yap about this to anyone. I don't want Sean or me dad to hear.'

'Cross my heart and hope to die,' said Smiler solemnly.

At home, luckily, only Granny was in, pressing Dad's shirt with one of the two heavy irons heating on the range. When she saw Ben's face she put down the iron. 'What's wrong, pet?'

She listened quietly. Though cross with him for what she called 'stupid messing', she swung into action and insisted Ben accompany her straight away to Billy's and to Mickser's houses. 'We've got to get this sorted before your dad or Sean get home,' she said. 'Better keep it quiet.'

Mrs Flynn gave out yards to her son Billy, whom she sarcastically called 'yer man, the football champion', while Mrs Woolfson needed some persuasion that her Maurice could have been mixed up in any wrongdoing. Eventually they both agreed to pay five shillings towards the cost next pay-day, which, with Smiler's contribution, left Ben with five shillings to earn.

Going back down the street, Granny said, 'I'm not happy about deceiving your dad, Ben, but he has a lot of worries. That old man's a decent skin to pay out for the window after what you lot did, and you have to pay your share.' She sighed. 'And there's no money to spare here. Sean and Uncle Matt help out, but ...'

Ben knew Dad was going 'down the pub for a few jars' more frequently these days, 'trying to drown his worries in drink,' as he'd heard Uncle Matt mutter to Granny. At least, now, Ben finally had a kind of a job, though he couldn't use the money for Mam, at least not for quite a while.

'Sorry, Granny,' he murmured. 'You going to tell Mam?'

'No need to worry her.' She pushed open the door and they went back into the kitchen, still hot from the ironing. 'Anyway,' she went on, 'like Marie said, that family next door are harmless enough.' She sank into the ancient *súgán* chair, looking suddenly old.

'Will I make you a cup of tea?' Ben offered. She nodded, and taking a spoonful of used tea leaves from the basin in the scullery he put them to steep in boiling water in the mug to squeeze out every last bit of strength, added milk from the press, a half spoon of sugar, stirred it and handed it to her.

'Grand cup of tea,' she said, smiling. 'Good thing you know how to light a fire as well.'

* * *

Soon after Dad and Sean had left for work the next Saturday morning, Ben, checking no one was around to spot him, knocked on the green door of Number 17. His stomach knotted up at the thought of entering the alien house forbidden by his dad, and meeting that strange girl again.

He was let in by the father, in his best suit, who clearly didn't know what he was there for.

Ben muttered, 'Er, I'm …'

Feet thumped down the stairs and Mabel, plump and cheery-looking, hairbrush in hand, appeared in the tiny hallway. She looked surprised. 'Aren't you–' she paused, 'from next door?' He nodded. The father quickly disappeared upstairs.

With difficulty Ben forced out, 'Er, I've come to light the fire … your granda …' Her mother appeared behind the girl. She had the same open, rosy face as the daughter, and a soft, motherly double chin. She stared at him for a moment. 'Oh yes,' she said then. 'Zaida said you'd come.' Zaida must be the granda. Funny name, he thought.

And then he looked up to see the younger girl descending the stairs with a plump, fair-haired baby in her arms and the puppy at her heels. She stopped dead at the sight of Ben. He saw again the mass of dark curly hair, the thin tense face, the arresting blue gaze, the scowl.

'Zaida sent him,' said Mabel. 'He's the new *Shabbos goy*. I'm Mabel,' she introduced herself, 'and this is Hetty.' As he'd expected, Hetty glared at him.

Ben knew he should say something about the puppy, but couldn't think what, even when it jumped up excitedly and barked a welcome. 'Come here, Mossy,' snapped Hetty. Her mother took the baby, who smiled at Ben and dribbled and waved his little fat hands about.

In a friendly tone, Mabel asked Ben his name. When he told her she seemed surprised. 'Ben? Short for Benjamin? But that's a Jewish name!'

'Oh no,' he protested, startled. 'It's short for Benedict. He was my granda, though I didn't know him.'

There was a brief silence. Then Mabel said: 'Right, well, I'd better get ready for the synagogue. Zaida's warned us not to be late.'

'Hetty, show Ben what's what while I dress Solly,' said their mother.

Ungraciously, Hetty brought newspaper, kindling and matches, and showed Ben the woven basket to be refilled with the turf stacked to dry in the passage outside the kitchen, and the pile of logs in the yard.

Back inside there was a tap at the front window and Hetty opened the door for Zaida.

'I thought I'd call by for you to make sure you're all on time! Ah!' he said genially at the sight of Ben, 'the brand new *Shabbos goy*.' He turned to Hetty, 'I can smell your Ma's cholent cooking right out in the street.' Ben, who'd also noticed the delicious smell, felt his stomach rumble and wondered what on earth a 'cholent' was.

'It's a stew with dumplings that we have for the

Sabbath,' Zaida told him, as if Ben had spoken aloud. 'Maybe you'll stay and have some.' Hetty looked up sharply, and Zaida added hastily, 'Or maybe another time.'

Ben smiled weakly, wishing they would all go and let him get on with his task and get home quickly. And they finally did go, all in a flurry, and he was alone with a sleeping dog in the empty, alien house.

* * *

Ben, thankful he knew how to light a fire properly from the Wolf Hound Patrol at school, knelt down before the hearth, carefully brushing out the clouds of powdery ash with the brush and pan. He crumpled sheets of newspaper into balls and placed them in the grate, criss-crossing thin sticks on top, and finally clods of turf from the basket.

Striking a match, he lit the paper spills. The tiny blue and gold flame ate its way into the paper, slowly then faster, until the sticks lit up with crackling sparks which died down when they met the heavy, damp turf. Ben grabbed the bellows, pumping them violently till the turf began to smoulder, filling the room with clouds of smoke that made his eyes water.

After a few minutes, he added a couple of logs, waiting patiently until they too caught fire, the smoke thinned and the warm rose-gold flames leaped in the polished grate.

Ben put back the fireguard, pocketed the two pence left for him on the mantelpiece, and with enormous relief slipped out the front door and back to the safety of Number 19. He went straight up to his bedroom and took out the shoebox he had hidden under the bed. He would save all his earnings in it until he had the five shillings to repay the old man.

* * *

On Sunday after tea, seated on the unsteady stool in his and Sean's freezing bedroom labouring over his arithmetic homework, he chewed the end of his pen, recalling Saturday morning.

When Granny'd asked about the Goldens' house, he'd told her that the wooden kitchen chairs, the shiny patterned oilcloth covering the table, and the row of white mugs hanging from hooks on the dresser were like their own, except there was a battered armchair in place of their own *súgán* chair by the fire.

But on the walls, instead of the Sacred Heart lamp and pictures of Our Lady or the Pope or St Martin de Porres – who, it was said, never refused a request – there was a tinted print of an ancient city with domes and walls of golden stone. In the parlour were photographs of family groups in long, old-fashioned clothes. An old man with a white beard, wearing a captain's hat, had a commanding look – not unlike Hetty's that day at the canal. His plump wife sat beside him, her hair in a plait around her head, holding a solemn baby wrapped in a lace shawl, probably a grandchild; other adults and children sat or stood together, all gazing at the camera with serious intensity.

And on the table he'd noticed a pile of heavy black books, the titles printed in gold in a weird script that definitely wasn't English.

So, in a way Number 17 was the same as their home, yet it was also strange and different …

Then, thinking of Monday morning, and the trouble he'd get into for not doing his homework, he firmly switched his mind back to his sums.

6

The Sanatorium

The ball came zooming down towards Ben out of the damp, misty afternoon air. He tensed his body and ran to meet it, putting all his strength into the kick. The ball flew from the scuffed toe of his boot, curved in a wide arc, bounced sideways on the uneven setts of the street and, amazingly, rolled between the two bundled-up jackets, to the fury of burly Billy Flynn, Sean's friend, who'd made the wrong judgement and leapt high in the air.

A cheer went up and Smiler, his face aglow, rushed over to pat Ben on the back. 'Grand shot!' Sean just gave him a grudging nod.

But even after that goal, Ben found it hard to concentrate, gnawed as he was by anxiety since the day last week when his Mam had been taken in an ambulance to Crooksling sanatorium. The house felt different, emptier. And now that Mam wasn't there to defend him, he had to be even more careful not to provoke his dad.

The previous day, in Kevin Street library, where his mother used to take them to borrow books, he'd looked up TB, learning that the real name of Mam's illness was tuberculosis, but people feared even using the word, often calling it 'consumption'. One time he'd heard

Granny explaining to a neighbour that Mam was delicate, with a weak chest.

Although the book didn't say so, everyone knew that having a family member with TB was a disgrace for the whole family, partly because it was contagious. Ben wondered how his mam had caught it. Who could be to blame for bringing this awful disease that had reduced his lively mother – full of laughter and opinions, the only person who could tease Dad out of his black moods – to such weakness?

On the day before she was taken in, Ben had seen her white pillow stained scarlet after a coughing fit. From that moment, a sharp sliver of fear had entered his heart like the blade of a knife, and never left.

Still, Granny had told him and Sean that Mam would have proper treatment in the sanatorium, and they must all pray for her.

'She'll come home a new woman,' Dad had said, too heartily. But Ben missed her badly.

* * *

Then one morning at breakfast, Granny, holding the toasting fork with a thick slice of bread out to the fire, turned to him. 'Ben, pet, would you like to come and see your mam?'

His heart leapt. 'I thought children weren't allowed?'

'Well, Uncle Matt knows the ward nurse,' said Granny. 'But we'd have to stay outside because of infection.'

The following Sunday after early Mass, Ben and Granny walked in the rain through Kevin Street, past the Meath hospital to wait with the crowd at Aston Quay for the Wicklow bus.

Beneath the low granite wall the waters of the Liffey slid sluggishly, like dark curds, under the arches of O'Connell bridge. Opposite, McBirney's usually bustling store was enveloped in a Sunday hush.

When the bus arrived the crowd climbed on, Ben and Granny carrying a basket with goodies for Mam: freshly made scones, a wedge of cheese, fresh eggs supplied by a neighbour from the chickens in her back yard, and sweet, shrivelled apples from the orchards of the big houses in Bloomfield Avenue where, Ben knew, Sean and his friends had gone 'boxing the fox' a few weeks earlier.

Granny fished in her purse to pay the uniformed conductor. When he'd clipped two tickets in the machine slung round her neck she pulled out her rosary beads and closed her eyes, muttering prayers under her breath, until, still clutching the beads, she nodded off.

Ben wiped his steamed-up glasses and stared out of the mud-splashed windows at fields scarred with frost, the leafless skeletons of the trees, and in the distance the rising Wicklow hills, their peaks scalloped with snow. He was torn between longing to see Mam and dread of seeing her in this alarming place.

But instead of a forbidding stone building like the TB hospital in Rialto, here white-coated nurses and patients were walking between pretty, cottage-style buildings and a small church, set in grassy slopes dotted with tall pine trees.

They walked through dim green corridors, past holy statues and people knitting, fingering rosary beads, or staring out the windows. Ben, anxious, knew he wasn't supposed to be inside.

As they entered Mam's ward he clutched Granny's hand and nervously scanned the patients, lying prone or with curtains drawn around their beds. But a nurse quickly ushered them out to a long veranda with only a wooden roof and back wall for shelter. And there, in the chill air, in one of the ranks of iron beds covered with oil sheets against the rain, was his mother.

* * *

To his relief, she was sitting up, wearing her shawl, scarf and woolly mittens, a vivid pink glow in her cheeks, a welcoming smile making her thin face beautiful. Although she couldn't hug them, her voice was strong.

She was thrilled to see Ben. 'How are you, Benny love?' she said, smiling. 'I think you've grown taller!' Ben was tongue-tied, and just gazed at her, smiling too.

Mam was hungry for news from home, and they gave her all the family news. '... and Sean sends love, and Matt'll be out to see you Sunday,' said Granny.

'Grand,' said Mam. There was a pause. Then Granny added awkwardly, 'Er, I expect Stephen'll be out as soon as he ...'

Mam's face clouded. 'Ah sure, it's hard for him, seeing me here like this–'

'He misses you,' Granny said.

'I know he does.' With an effort, she asked brightly, 'Tell me, any word of young Paddy?'

'He's fine,' said Granny. 'He's with the convoys, bringing back supplies from America for the war effort.' She sighed. 'Of course, Matt and Bridie worry about him. But he wanted to go.'

'You'd worry about anyone caught up in this terrible war.'

Breaking the silence that followed, Gran told her, 'Matt's busy with the protest.'

Ben brightened. He knew all about this from his uncle. 'It's against the wage-cuts and the anti-trade union Bill,' he explained to Mam. 'Big Jim Larkin's speaking.'

'They're expecting thousands up in College Green,' added Granny.

'I just hope something comes of it,' said Mam. 'Prices shooting up and thousands out of work–' She gave a hoarse cough.

Noting her worried look, Granny changed the subject. 'By the way, I told Stephen I met our new neighbour, Mrs Golden, a nice woman.'

'I s'pose he wasn't pleased,' said Mam, with a rueful grin.

Granny said with a sniff, 'Well, no – but I told him, they *are* neighbours.'

Mam nodded, and turned to Ben. 'And what are you up to, Benny love?'

'Nothing much, Mam.' He'd have liked to tell her how the cross girl with whom he'd saved the puppies was now living next door. But Dad might hear, and get angry. He'd tell her the whole story when she was home again. She'd be really proud of him for the rescue, and for becoming a *Shabbos goy* and working for money. But Granny had said not to worry her about anything.

Trying to stop his voice trembling he asked, 'When d'you think you'll ...?'

'Oh, I'll be out of here very soon,' said Mam brightly.

'Please God,' said Granny.

'Just let them try and keep me here,' said Mam. They all grinned, and Ben's heart lightened.

Looking around the veranda at the patients bundled up in shawls and coats, Ben asked, 'Why's everyone out here in the cold?'

'They say it's best for' – his mam hesitated – 'for the

disease. You need clean air and sunshine.' She smiled. 'There's plenty of fresh air, all right.'

In the next bed sat a fragile young girl, her skin pale and clear as marble with a hectic rosy spot on each cheek. Granny, handing around the food, included her. She took a scone and nibbled it. Smiling at them, she said, 'Me family are having novenas said for me.' She gave a series of staccato coughs. 'Me ma's sure it'll help.'

As she talked on feverishly about her brothers and sisters, all living in two damp rooms in a tenement, she smoothed back her fine hair, like spun gold. Ben had a recollection of old Granny Murphy, who used to live next door, saying grimly of a sick child from the street, 'Consumption has no pity for blue eyes and golden hair.'

'She's only Sean's age, God love her,' Mam murmured to Granny with a sigh.

But surely, thought Ben, both his Mam and the girl would get better, now they were in the sanatorium?

When they said goodbye Ben felt a choking lump in his throat. As they headed away down the veranda past the rows of beds, Mam called hoarsely: 'Goodbye, Mam. Goodbye, me darling boy. Give my best love to Dad and Sean,' and as she blew them kisses, like before her white hand appeared to Ben like a fluttering bird, rising and falling, but unable to fly.

* * *

Chugging home in the bus, Granny, aware of Ben's sadness, produced from the basket a well-thumbed copy of
the *Reader's Digest*, the little magazine passed on to her
every month by a neighbour. 'There, pet, have a read of
that,' she said. 'There's usually something interesting in it.'

Listlessly, Ben leafed through it. Soon he was deep in
an article about eating nutritious foods and vitamins to
build up strength, especially, it said, after an illness.

He told Granny, 'When Mam gets back, we should get
her the right food–'

'We should, Ben.' Her forehead creased in a frown.
'But there's not much money to spare. Wages might be
cut – and Christmas is coming.'

Seeing his crestfallen look she added quickly, 'Sure,
we'll do what we can.' And she got out her knitting, a
familiar grey knee-sock with a brown pattern around the
turnover top, which, now that Sean wore long trousers,
Ben knew was intended for him. As she knitted she
hummed her favourite song, 'The Last Rose of Summer',
which she used to sing as a child on the farm in Meath
where she grew up. Whenever he or Sean grumbled
about having to do jobs around the house Granny would
silence them with stories about getting up at four in the
morning to milk the cows, deliver the milk and help with
the younger children and the breakfast, all before a

three-mile walk to school – hail, rain or snow.

As rain spattered the bus window, Ben watched her small, liver-spotted hands with knobbly joints flashing the pink knitting needles in and out. His head fell forward, and, dozing, he pictured again the scene he had revisited before: the Golden girl, Hetty, her face grim with determination, pulling him back across the ice.

* * *

At home, Dad was heaping turf on the kitchen fire. He turned and said unexpectedly to Ben, 'I see visiting Mam did you good!' He touched Ben's shoulder comfortingly. 'Let's hope she's home for Christmas.'

If only Dad could always be like this, Ben thought, like he often used to be, then he could stop feeling afraid of him.

Later, Granny, bemoaning shortages of sugar and the lack of candied fruit and brandy, enlisted Sean and Ben's help in making the Christmas pudding. As they stirred and sampled the tasty mix, Sean said, carelessly, 'Shame about that cake though, from next door.' Ben stopped stirring.

'What cake?' asked Granny.

'Er, the young wan from next door brought it in,' muttered Sean as Dad glared at him. 'Something to do with their festival, she said.'

'And where is it?' asked Granny grimly.

'I sent it back,' grunted Dad. 'We don't need *their* charity.'

Granny raised her eyes to heaven. 'They meant well, Stephen,' she chided Dad. 'No need to throw it back at them.'

Dad scowled, his moment of softness over. 'I'm off out,' he barked, banging the door after him.

Granny tied string around the pudding basin, ready for steaming. Ben felt uncomfortable about the cake. He hoped it had been the older girl, Mabel, who'd brought it. If it was Hetty, he could picture all too clearly her blue eyes blazing with anger.

7

The Festival of Lights

That Sunday morning, while Ben and Granny were on their way to the sanatorium, Hetty was bathing Solly in the galvanised iron bath in front of the kitchen fire. It was a task she actually enjoyed, though she'd never have admitted it.

'Hospital Requests' was playing on the big Pye wireless of polished wood that Da had bought last year after a rare win at the races. It cost eight guineas new and Ma wasn't pleased. She thought the money should have been put aside as savings. Count John McCormack was singing a poignant song, 'Panis Angelicus', which Hetty knew her da would make her switch off if he came in – because it was Christian, he would say, 'not our religion'.

Firmly gripping the baby's slippery pink body, she rubbed him with a soapy rag, avoiding splashes from his waving arms. Hearing Solly's gurgles, Mossy pattered across the wet floor, wagging his stumpy tail.

'Wait, Mossy,' said Hetty in a gentle tone she reserved solely for puppies and babies. 'I'll feed you when I've finished with Solly.'

Da had said the puppies' survival was thanks to the mercy of the Almighty. Ma said it was also due to Hetty's devoted care. But Hetty knew in her heart that the courage of 'that boy' had been the vital factor. She was secretly grateful to him, but, of course, would never dream of showing it.

When Ma'd insisted they could keep one puppy only, there'd been a row during which Hetty had rushed away with the two puppies in her arms and flung herself and them on her bed, displacing an annoyed Mabel. Finally the other puppy, Flossy, had been given to cousin Eddie, the only person Hetty trusted to look after it properly.

Tonight was the last night of Hanukkah – the Festival of Lights – and her grandparents, together with Aunt Millie, Uncle Sam and Eddie, were all coming to Martin Street for the festival.

Aunt Millie always helped prepare the special festive meals, and she and Mabel had gone to Lombard Street West to choose from the fresh fish displayed by the dealers on wooden boards balanced on prams. They would also bring back delicious foods from Ordman's shop in Clanbrassil Street, including Zaida's favourite pickled cucumbers swimming in dillweed. Aunt Millie insisted, as usual, on paying for everything as she knew money was scarce in the Martin Street household.

This too was the night for Hanukkah presents. As Hetty dried Solly on a strip of old sheet on her lap, she reflected gloomily that, while presents in their family had always been modest, this year there probably would be none at all.

Last week their Da, usually at work long hours in the tailoring shop or wrapped up in his books, had gone off to the bookie's at Kelly's Corner and spent part of his much-needed weekly wage betting on the horses.

When Ma'd tried to stop him, he insisted, 'This time I've got a real cert.' His excited, agitated manner at these times was familiar to them all. On his way out he was still repeating, 'I'm telling you, Sarah, this one can't lose.'

But as they could see when he returned much later, all the animation drained away and replaced by an equally familiar hangdog look, it did lose.

'More money down the drain,' Hetty had hissed to her sister that night.

Mabel was in tears. 'Ma promised to get a few yards of taffeta for a new dress for Eddie's Barmitzvah party and for the hop at Carlisle – if I get asked,' she moaned. 'How can I go to anything now? I've nothing to wear.' Dabbing her eyes with a corner of the sheet, she went on: 'Why won't they let me leave that stupid school? I mean, I'm nearly sixteen. I could be earning.'

'Bobba says education helps you make something of yourself,' Hetty reminded her. 'She always says she wishes she'd had the chance.'

'Grown-ups always say those things.'

'D'you remember Zaida saying everything would be better here in Martin Street?' Hetty brushed her teeth vigorously with a handful of salt from the dish beside the basin. 'Well, it isn't. Not with Da, anyway.'

Mabel, who never remained upset for long, sat up. 'Some things *are* better here,' she said, blowing her nose. 'Those two girls up the street, Carmel and Maureen, asked me to go to the pictures with them, except they usually go on Saturday. And that boy in the synagogue last week – he was gorgeous.' She went over to the mirror propped on a stool, which served as a dressing table, and fluttered her eyelashes at her reflection. Dreamily she said, 'Did I tell you he came over and shook hands and said "*Shabbat Shalom*"?'

'Only about twenty times,' groaned Hetty. 'And everyone says that after the service anyway – it only means "Have a peaceful Sabbath"!'

'He's called Michael,' Mabel continued, oblivious. 'He might ask me to the hop. And guess what? He's a medical student!'

'Oh great!' said Hetty acidly. 'And I s'pose the half-a-jar of greasy Brylcreem on his hair's for medical reasons?'

Mabel ignored her, gazing around their bedroom, more lived-in now, with flimsy curtains and film star photos up on the wall, a flowery rug crocheted by their grandmother on the bare lino, a wind-up alarm clock on the mantelpiece.

'You've got to admit,' she said to Hetty, 'there's one good thing about Martin Street – our own room.'

As Hetty nodded grudgingly, there was a scratching at the door. Brightening, she flew to open it, and gathered up the puppy into her arms. As he devoured her with slobbering licks, she said, 'And there's Mossy, too.'

'Mmm,' said Mabel, patting him absently. 'Hetty, y'know Ben, the new *Shabbos goy*?' Ignoring Hetty's stony expression, she went on: 'He hardly talks when we see him. Hasn't he even asked you about the puppies?'

Hetty shrugged. 'They're strange people next door.' She'd been so close to Ben on the canal bank. But now if she saw him in the street he looked away, and so did she. She wasn't going to admit to Mabel that she couldn't forget that day on the ice and his sympathy when she'd wept. Still, maybe he really didn't care?

And anyway, she scolded herself, why was she, Hetty, even thinking about him? Why was she hurt by his indifference? Hetty always ignored boys, except Eddie, of course, and sneered at Mabel and the others for their stupid chat about boyfriends. Why did her thoughts now keep returning to this boy? Hetty was confused, and a little bit ashamed of herself. She *must* put him out of her mind.

Determinedly, she climbed into bed, and cuddling

Mossy to her, resolutely opened her library book, *Anne of Green Gables*, and settled down to read.

* * *

Later that Sunday morning, having dressed Solly and put him in his cot for a rest, Hetty was sitting with twenty other boys and girls at the old scored wooden desks in the classroom in Zion Schools, its musty, chalky smell mingling with the pungent odour of fresh varnish.

After being stuck in school the whole week, Hetty resented Sunday Hebrew classes.

Beside her one of the boys was stumbling through his English translation of the Hebrew Old Testament. On her other side, Gertie, the closest Hetty had to a best friend, was following her book. Hetty stared longingly out of the high windows at the expanse of blue sky and racing clouds above the houses in Bloomfield Avenue.

At least she was avoiding the flurry of cooking and cleaning for the visitors. Aunt Millie, her mother and Mabel would be busily mincing fish, mixing it with egg and crumbly matzo meal and seasoning to make *gefilte* fish, served with extra strong red horseradish sauce that made your eyes water.

Hetty brightened up when the teacher, Reverend Roth, switched from Hebrew study to the story of the Hanukkah festival. In spite of herself she got caught up in the dramatic tale of the heroic Jewish leader Judah Maccabeus, who in ancient times led an army to recapture the holy temple in Jerusalem, destroyed by their enemies. Although there was only enough holy oil to light the everlasting flame for one day, through a miracle it had lasted for eight days, burning brighter every day. 'And so,' the teacher finished, 'even in the dark days of Jewish defeat and exile, the flame was kept alight.'

He closed the book. 'Who can tell me how we celebrate this miracle?'

'We start with one candle and light an extra one each night,' a boy said.

To speed things up, Hetty added, 'So tonight there'll be eight candles burning together.'

'Good,' said the teacher. 'Happy Hanukkah!' The class finished with a rousing chorus of the Hanukkah song, *Ma'oz Tsur* – Rock of my Salvation – sung at top speed. Finally, after a prayer for fellow Jews and all victims of Nazi persecution, the class was over.

* * *

'Who's ready for potato *latkes?*' asked Ma that evening, her face flushed amid the talk and laughter around the crowded table. 'Or should we light the Hanukkah candles first?'

Uncle Sam groaned. 'We've all eaten too much.

73

Anyway, we should do the candles first.' He turned to Ma. 'Sarah, the *gefilte* fish was wonderful.'

'All due to Millie!' said Ma, gathering up the plates.

'Maybe Leon should let out our waistbands,' joked Zaida.

'No-one gets rich letting out trousers,' snapped Bobba. Jokes were not her strong point. 'It's time he moved on from buttonholes to something that pays better.'

'All clothes need buttonholes,' Ma put in quickly. 'It's a skill.'

Bobba sniffed. 'There's better skills.' Listening, Hetty reflected that Bobba, a tiny woman with thinning flossy pale curls and soft skin like a peach, was a lot sharper than she appeared.

Hetty and Eddie were trying to play a game of draughts on the rug in front of the fire, interrupted by Mossy sniffing hopefully at the pieces, and by Solly trying to grab them and put them in his mouth. With relief, she could see that her parents appeared to be back on speaking terms. After the loss at the bookie's, Ma had been tight-lipped for almost a week. She glanced at her sister, laboriously sewing a deep lace frill around the hem of a dress passed on to her last year by her school friend Alison, unfortunately a good few inches shorter than Mabel, and much thinner.

The family would muddle along till Da did it again, she

thought. But there was the higher rent, due every Friday. Thank goodness Ma got help from Zaida and Uncle Sam, and that Millie was so generous with food, especially for the Sabbath and the important festivals.

'Your turn, Hetty,' said Eddie. 'You're not concentrating.' As the baby made a grab for his iron leg-brace, stuck awkwardly out in front of him, Eddie picked him up, swinging him in the air so that he gurgled in delight.

'*Now* who's not concentrating,' said Hetty triumphantly as she overtook three of his pieces with her king, laughing at Eddie's groans.

* * *

'What are the neighbours like?' Aunt Millie enquired as she helped Ma to clear the table.

'There's a pleasant old couple on one side,' replied Ma. Then, as they carried plates into the deep stone sink in the scullery, she lowered her voice, 'But the people the other side, the Byrnes, are a puzzle ...'

Hetty, sent in by Da to find the box of Bo-Peep matches for the candle-lighting, stopped to listen. 'The old lady's nice – I met her out shopping – and there's two boys,' Ma said. 'The younger boy's our *Shabbos goy*, but he doesn't say much. And the father never gives so much as a nod. I believe the mother's in hospital.'

'That must be hard,' said Aunt Millie.

'Yes, poor woman. I sent in some milky cake, just made this morning.' She smiled. 'I even sieved some coarse flour through a stocking, to make it white!'

I hope she washed the stocking, thought Hetty. Aloud she said casually, 'Who left it in?'

'Mabel gave it to the older boy.'

Hetty wondered if they'd had it for their tea. Maybe Ben would be sent in to thank them. She might even remind him about the rescue, and he might become more friendly. That made her unaccountably pleased.

In the parlour, Da, mindful of shortages, selected a single match. Squeezed together in the small room they lit all the candles, each taking a turn. According to custom, Zaida placed the flickering menorah by the window and recited the prayer. They belted out the Hanukkah song with mock-reproachful looks towards Da when he sang, as usual, painfully out of tune. 'Throat needs a drop of oil,' murmured Zaida, as he always did.

Bobba sang one of the verses alone, her voice cracked but still sweet, the frown lines in her face relaxed, and in the soft candlelight they could see for a moment how she might have been as a striking, determined young woman, uprooted from her home in Poland, having to cope with hardship in an alien land.

Later they ate the *latkes* – crispy fried potato pancakes dipped in apple sauce – along with tea for the grown-ups and lemonade for the children. Then the wireless was turned on for the six o'clock news.

Further rationing of clothes and essentials in Ireland were announced, and Irish town dwellers were asked to help the severe fuel shortage by volunteering to cut turf on the bogs.

Mabel whispered to Hetty that it sounded fun, but she guessed they'd never be allowed. 'I've heard it's harder than you'd think,' muttered Eddie. He grinned ruefully, glancing down at his withered leg. '*I* wouldn't be much use anyway.' His mother reached out and touched his shoulder. 'There are plenty of other things you can do well, dear.'

Listening to the news, the adults, as usual, discussed the plight of the Jews in Europe.

Hetty burst out, 'In Hebrew classes we learned that a rabbi said: "If I am not for myself, who will be for me? If I am for myself alone, what am I? And if not now, when?" It meant we must stand up for ourselves and also help other people in trouble, and do it now, not put it off.'

They looked at her, surprised at the outburst. Da frowned, but Uncle Sam said, 'Yes, a rabbi did say that.'

Da put in, 'It's not so simple–'

'Why?' asked Hetty defiantly. 'We could start by following up the rumours of that refugee girl Eddie heard about and try and help her.' As Eddie nodded approvingly, she went on, her voice rising, 'It's no good just sitting here doing nothing.'

'Now, Hetty!' said Ma warningly.

Hetty ignored her. 'After all, we're all here only because Zaida and Bobba came as refugees and were able to stay.'

'Don't answer back to your elders,' snapped Da. He turned to Bobba and Zaida. 'She thinks she knows everything.'

Bobba said quietly, 'Hetty may be lacking in respect, but she spoke the truth.'

'I know what it is to be uprooted,' agreed Zaida. 'People who've always lived in the same place don't realise how hard it is to make a new life. And it's much harder for refugees to stay here now than when I came years ago.'

'In Northern Ireland there's a farm for young Jewish refugees at Millisle in County Down,' said Uncle Sam. 'And we've set up a Refugee Aid Committee here to help the Belfast people raise funds for them.'

'That's all very well, Sam,' Bobba put in, 'but how do you find any refugees who got to Dublin?'

'This country's neutral in this war and we have to be careful to stay within the law,' said Uncle Sam.

Hetty thought about the poor girl people said was somewhere in Dublin. She decided that she would not wait around for all this talking and planning and being careful. She would DO something even if it got her into trouble.

Ma finally stopped all the war talk and argument, saying, 'It's time for the Hanukkah presents.'

The presents were a surprise, due mainly, everyone knew, to their aunt and uncle. Hetty got a little brightly painted wooden weather house, with a boy and girl in the doorway. 'We got it in Switzerland before the war,' said Aunt Millie, smiling. 'When the weather's going to be fine, the girl comes out–'

'And when it's bad, the boy comes out,' finished Hetty.

'That's not fair,' interrupted Eddie. 'Why's the boy the one to show the bad weather?'

'That's just the way it is,' said Hetty sweetly, flinging her arms around her aunt. 'It's lovely. I'll keep it on the mantelpiece in our room.'

Eddie received a new chessboard, and Solly a toy rabbit with floppy ears made by Bobba from oddments of material. They all got a hug and kiss and a shilling from Zaida. But happiest of all was Mabel, presented by her aunt and uncle with a length of sky-blue taffeta for a new dress.

As they left, Hetty stepped out into the sharp cold of the street. Turning to go back inside, she heard a footstep and saw a boy standing on the path. At last, she thought, it's him! And her heart jumped in a peculiar way. But then she saw, in the deepening dusk, that it was a different boy, taller and older – the brother.

Silently, he held out a package. Not sure what it was, she took it.

Sounding embarrassed, he choked out, 'Er, sorry, Da said we don't need this, thanks.' And he turned and hurried back next door.

She pulled off the paper. It was her mother's milky cake.

8

Christmas

'What're you getting for Christmas?' asked Smiler. He and Ben were squeezed into Smiler's tiny bedroom poring over his stamp collection. Licking a hinge, Smiler carefully secured to the page his new Irish halfpenny stamp with the Sword of Light picture. Smiler went on, 'I'm getting a new stamp album, and Granda *might* give me some money for the bike.' Smiler had been saving for months for a bike to replace the wreck he'd inherited from three older brothers, but the five shillings he'd paid for the broken window set him back a lot and he was nowhere near having enough money even for the second-hand bike he longed for.

'Don't know what *I'm* getting,' said Ben gloomily. He was living in hope that Mam might be home for Christmas. Before she was sick she used to save small sums over the year for Christmas presents. One year his dad had carved a wooden model boat for them which they called the *Lady Marie*, and they'd all gone to sail it on the canal on St Stephen's Day.

If he could help Mam get well, he told himself, maybe Christmas would be like it used to be. He'd prayed to Our Lady, as Granny advised, hoping for an extra job at Christmastime.

But jobs were hard to find. He helped Smiler with his paper round, and carried sacks of potatoes for an elderly neighbour. Now it was a week before Christmas, money was scarce, and he hadn't even got a Christmas present ready for Mam's homecoming.

* * *

But Mam didn't get home for Christmas; she was still in Crooksling. Ben pictured her sitting up in bed on the veranda wrapped in her shawl, the golden-haired girl beside her, thinking about them all. She hadn't even been well enough for visits, but Granny and Dad told the boys she was improving.

Ben and Sean together had sent her a bottle of Bourjois Californian Poppy perfume from Woolworth's, and she sent woollen mufflers she'd knitted for them, and cards with loving messages. Still, if only he could see her...

'Hurry up, Ben, we'll be late,' called Granny from downstairs. Transferring his favourite conker into the pocket of his good trousers, Ben clumped down the stairs.

In the hall, ready for their annual Christmas Eve visit to Uncle Matt's, the family was waiting, all dickied up: Dad, only just back from Jacobs' biscuit factory's annual Christmas dinner with his workmates, 'with a few drinks on him', in Granny's words, uncomfortable in a white shirt and stiff collar; a scrubbed-looking Sean, hair slicked down with water; and Granny, her best shawl draped over layers of clothes, her button boots shining, a paisley-patterned scarf knotted around her wispy hair.

They were all acutely aware of the absence of Mam, in her velvet-collared coat – well past its best, as she always said wryly – who at this point would have inspected each of them with an approving word, before linking her arm in Dad's as they set off.

As they trooped out into the street Ben glanced at Number 17, but to his relief there was no one to be seen. It was bad enough being a secret *Shabbos goy*, but since Dad had sent back the cake he felt even more uncomfortable in the Goldens' house.

The street was alive with the shouts of children playing in the crisp wintry sunshine while mothers and sisters were busy with Christmas preparations. Two small girls twirled dizzily on a rope wound around a lamp post.

Ben stopped to talk to Smiler, sitting on the granite kerb trying to mend the ragged inner tube of his ancient bike. Inner tubes, along with tyres, were hard to find nowadays. 'You can only get them on the black market,' Sean told Smiler airily. 'Cost you a small fortune, though.' He lowered his voice. 'Smuggled over the border from the North.'

'Smuggled?' Smiler was impressed.

'Sure,' said Sean, with a superior air. 'And there's people from the North comin' down here buying clothes to beat the rationing.'

'How d'you know?' asked Ben. Since Sean had joined the ARP, he seemed to know everything.

Sean grinned. 'Didn't you hear about the fella who came down to Dublin in an oul' suit, bought a new one in Guiney's, and on the train back up he went to the jacks to change? He threw the old suit out the window so he wouldn't be caught with two, opened up the parcel from Guiney's' – Sean paused for dramatic effect – 'and then didn't yer man find that they'd left out the trousers!' He was laughing so much at his own joke he had to be called twice by his impatient father.

Further down the street a friend of Mam's came over to ask, 'How's herself?'

'Getting on,' said Granny, as she always said when asked this question.

Sean ran off to chat to Joey Woolfson, and a neighbour who worked with Dad stopped to remind him about the trade union protest after Christmas. 'Bring the young fellas,' he advised. 'Never too soon to learn to stand together.'

* * *

Ben usually enjoyed visiting Uncle Matt and jolly Auntie Bridie, who wore bright red lipstick and whose blond hair was thought – disapprovingly by Granny – to have been helped by a bottle of hair-bleach. Apart from that, Bridie was famous for her baking. She owned and ran a success-ful cake shop and could always be relied on to bring along delicious cakes for every occasion, even during the war.

Since their son Paddy had left, Ben called in more often after school to read the papers to his uncle, who fol-lowed the war news avidly. Having volunteered and been wounded in the Spanish Civil War, he reacted furiously against Hitler, and the Nazis and Fascists in Europe, and also the Blueshirts and other home-grown Nazi sympa-thisers in Ireland.

But today's visit, without their mother, had an air of sadness, the sheen of brightness and fun dulled and flat, even though Uncle Matt, cheerful and balding, welcomed them to the already full house with cups of Cream Soda from the Taylor Keith factory where he used to work, a treat that tasted, he always told them, like velvet on the tongue. Clay pipe in hand, he passed around bottles of Guinness to Dad and the other men, and small glasses of port for the women. Auntie Bridie and Granny anxiously exchanged news of Mam and Paddy. Then Uncle Matt shepherded the boys upstairs for the ritual visit to his beloved pet birds.

Mounting the stairs they could hear the familiar chir-
ruping and twittering, like an insistent dawn chorus.
Sean, who hated birds, put his nose into the back bedroom, grimaced, and backed off downstairs. But Ben,
always charmed by the exotic room his uncle had created
in the ordinary little house, went in, despite the smell.

An entire wall was lined with wooden cages,
handmade by Uncle Matt before his sight dimmed. Hopping from floor to perch, the linnets, canaries and gold-
finches warbled and trilled, their glossy plumage glowing
green and golden in the rays of sunlight streaking in
through the window.

Ben had once asked his uncle if it wasn't cruel to
imprison them in cages.

'Well, people are always saying that – your auntie and
Paddy included,' he replied. 'But I let them out in the
room sometimes. Anyway, look at them, lad – what do
you think?'

And indeed, whenever Ben saw them they were
preening or singing or splashing in a saucer of water, or
pecking greedily at their special food, thistledown – the
feathery down and the seeds from thistles gathered for
two pence a sack by the local children from the fields further along the canal, a job the younger children loved.
Ben often did it too in the summer holidays.

* * *

When Ben came downstairs, sandwiches of thick bread filled with tinned salmon, potted meat and egg were being served. In the kitchen children were playing jacks and marbles, and Sean and the older ones were greedily surveying the sherry trifle, about to be borne in proudly by Auntie Bridie in her precious cut-glass bowl. Ben's mouth watered at the sight of this sweet concoction of sherry-soaked sponge, red jelly, custard and cream – no red cherries, though, complained Auntie Bridie, not since the war had begun.

By this time the neat front parlour, crammed with relations, friends and neighbours, resounded with talk and laughter. As the evening drew on, everyone did their party piece – a song or a recitation, or they played the mouth organ or the tinny, upright piano with its yellowing ivory keys. Uncle Matt, as always, belted out his favourite song, 'I Dreamed I Saw Joe Hill Last Night', and Granny and her friend Josie sang 'Just a Song at Twilight' in high, quavering voices. And later the crowd roared out the chorus of 'A Nation Once Again'.

Ben recalled that as the night came to a close each year people would always beg his mother, slender in the floaty dress that he had watched her stitching: Marie, before you go, give us 'She Moved Through the Fair', and his mam would sing in her sweet, soaring voice, '... it will not be long, love, till our wedding day ...' bringing a tear to every eye while his father, smiling, watched her proudly.

* * *

The remains of the trifle arrived back in the kitchen and Ben and Sean and the others scraped the bowl clean. Through the doorway they could hear the clatter of cups and glasses, snatches of conversation and a few raised voices, fuelled by drink.

'And now they want to outlaw strikes–'

'The only way for us to fight for decent pay,' someone interrupted heatedly.

'Big Jim Larkin'll tell 'em at the protest,' said Uncle Matt firmly.

Then their Dad's voice, slightly slurred. 'And if any of these foreign refugees get in here, they'll make it worse, taking our jobs ...'

Ben listened carefully.

'They say they're refugees,' a plump woman in a fluffy sweater said through a mouthful of cake, 'but they could be spies!'

Her husband, a Guard, put down his pint. 'We know there's illegal refugees here in Dublin, so keep your eyes open.' He lowered his voice. 'The immigration fellas are after them – one's a young girl.'

The party was winding down. But as people started getting up to leave, Ben heard Uncle Matt declare, 'Chasing out the few poor sods who manage to get out of that Nazi hellhole – especially a young one – it's no credit to us.'

In the kitchen, Ben and Sean exchanged glances as Dad wandered through, unsteadily, on his way out to the privy. Ben ran upstairs to get Granny, knitting and chatting with her friend Josie amid the birds, now silenced for the night with cloths over their cages. On the way down he told them what he'd heard about refugees.

'Well, I can't see that it'd harm us to have some new blood,' said Granny. 'Immigrants can help build up a country – look at America!'

'But they might be spies,' put in Josie. 'You can't be too careful.'

As they put on their coats in the hallway, Auntie Bridie appeared with a heap of sandwiches wrapped in paper. 'Here, take these,' she said, 'they were only made fresh. Young fellas are always hungry.' She added a hunk of Christmas cake. Dad, flushed and beery, flung his arms around her, and she planted a red, lipsticky kiss on his cheek.

Uncle Matt handed the boys their presents – pocket-money for both of them, and for Ben, whose birthday was at Christmas, a tartan-covered autograph book with 'All my love to Ben' already written in it in Mam's familiar writing, though a little shaky, followed by a quote: 'Never send to know for whom the bell tolls, it tolls for thee.' Uncle Matt murmured, 'It's from one of our Paddy's schoolbooks that I showed her.'

'That was a lovely party, so it was,' said Granny.

'It's not the same without poor Marie,' said Auntie Bridie softly, kissing them all. 'Please God, she'll be home soon.'

As they walked home, boots clattering on the frosty cobbles, Dad put a hand on Ben's shoulder to steady himself. Unexpectedly, he ruffled Ben's hair affectionately, just like he used to before Mam got sick and his angry black moods seemed to take over almost entirely.

9

News of the Refugee

The next week, Eddie, looking very excited, called around early to Martin Street, before Ben's arrival on Saturday morning. When Hetty came downstairs, he silently beckoned her into the parlour. 'I'll follow you to the synagogue,' she called to Ma, as Eddie closed the door softly behind them.

'I've some news,' he whispered. 'You know that girl refugee who's on the run? I've an idea where she is.'

'Where? How did you find out? Can we ...?' Maybe, at last, they could actually do something to help, even rescue her.

'Keep your voice down,' muttered Eddie. 'When Da came back from the Refugee Committee, I heard him tell Ma the immigration authorities might be on to her. Her visa's run out, and she's to be deported.'

'What's her name?' demanded Hetty. 'How old is she? D'you know her address?'

'Hush,' murmured Eddie. 'I saw an address scribbled on Da's desk – St Patrick's Avenue or Square in Dalkey, no name though ...' He hesitated. 'Da won't like us interfering. I think the committee wants to find her and help–'

'But they'll take ages, with talk and meetings, and then

it'll be too late,' Hetty argued. 'Let's go to Dalkey and find her ourselves.' Increasingly excited, she went on, 'Tomorrow after Hebrew class, it's Mabel's turn to mind Solly. We'll say we want to get sea air–'

There was a sound from the living room. 'What's that?' hissed Hetty. 'I thought they'd all gone.'

Very quietly Eddie opened the door. Ben, with his back to them, was on his knees at the hearth, shovelling out the ash. When had he arrived? Eddie and Hetty exchanged anxious glances, but absorbed in his task he didn't appear to have heard them. Still, they'd have to be careful.

When Ben finally rose and turned around, his eyes met Hetty's accusing gaze. Then Hetty looked away and hurried upstairs. She was already annoyed with the Byrnes, though Zaida, surprisingly, had said there were worse things than sending back a cake. But, now, what if Ben *had* heard the secret?

Below she could hear Eddie chatting to Ben. When she descended they were talking about Eddie's favourite football team, Shamrock Rovers, which was also Ben's. 'I go with my Da to their matches at Milltown sometimes–' Eddie was saying, but Hetty interrupted. 'We're late,' she told him, almost pushing him out the door.

Over her shoulder, Eddie called goodbye to Ben.

* * *

At the synagogue Hetty's mind was not on her prayers. How had this girl got to Ireland – and to Dalkey? How must she feel, alone and on the run? If they found her, could they somehow shelter her in Martin Street?

Outside after the service all the talk among the young people, to Hetty's disgust, was about the hop that evening after the Sabbath. Mabel, with her friend Rebecca, was in the middle of a crowd of girls who twittered like surprised birds when Michael and a couple of his friends came over. Michael had invited Mabel to the hop and she was ecstatic.

Hetty stood stony-faced waiting for her parents and Zaida, with only faithful Gertie beside her. 'I'd love to go to the hop, wouldn't you?' whispered Gertie. But Hetty's mind was on how soon she could talk privately to Eddie about Dalkey. Knowing Hetty as she did, Gertie didn't expect an answer.

That evening the excitement mounted at Number 17. Mabel was finally decked out in the blue dress, complete with ribbons, frills and lace, pronounced 'beautiful' by her parents and '*shayn*' – the Yiddish equivalent – by Bobba and Zaida. Yuk! was Hetty's silent comment, but no one asked her opinion.

Mabel's friends Carmel and Maureen called round to see her dressed up, and upstairs in the bedroom Carmel surreptitiously offered her a tiny box of lip rouge to put on when she got to the hop, which she'd have to rub off before she got home in case Da noticed.

Then Michael arrived, with a flower in his buttonhole and a box of Mackintosh's Double Centre Chocolate Toffee Assortment for Mabel. Da shook his hand and quickly disappeared upstairs, leaving Ma trying to make conversation. Mabel blushed and giggled; everyone except Hetty kept smiling, and Michael patted his waved hair.

Hetty finally escaped to the kitchen where she fed Solly chicken soup and mashed potato, most of which he happily dribbled out again.

When Gertie arrived, Hetty rushed her up to the bedroom before she could have a proper look at Mabel's dress. Gertie was disappointed. 'I came over to see them off.'

'See them off?' snorted Hetty. 'They're not getting married!'

'Not yet,' Gertie put in coyly.

'Come on,' said Hetty, 'let's have a game of rummy.'

'Honestly, Hetty!' Gertie's pretty face was puzzled as Hetty dealt the cards. 'I don't think you have a romantic bone in your body.'

'Just as well,' retorted Hetty. 'Mabel's romantic enough for both of us.'

But to please Gertie, they went downstairs and as the couple left, Hetty, catching Ma's eye, forced a smile and mumbled through gritted teeth, 'Have a nice time.'

Gertie went home too, and as the front door shut behind them all Hetty heaved an exaggerated sigh of relief and waited impatiently till Eddie arrived to plan their day by the sea.

10

The Spy

But Ben *had* overheard the discussion about the refugee. On that damp, chilly Saturday morning as he'd started on the fire, glad he was wearing Sean's old Aran jumper under his thin jacket, he'd heard sounds from the parlour. Surely the family had gone to the synagogue? Then he recognised the voices of Hetty and Eddie, lowered but still audible through the thin wooden door.

They were discussing a refugee on the run from police and immigration authorities, and making plans to search for her in Dalkey and hide her in Portobello! As he listened, Ben's mind flashed back to the talk of spies at Uncle Matt's at Christmas. But surely this girl couldn't be a spy?

The door opened suddenly. Without turning round, Ben carefully hung the poker and tongs back on the brass stand. After a few seconds the fire flamed up and he rose, chatted to Eddie, then took his payment from the mantelpiece and turned to leave.

For a second his eyes met Hetty's before she headed upstairs. Her gaze was fierce and determined and at first he thought she suspected him, but then he recognised that passionate expression – just like with the puppies, he recalled, except this time she was focused on saving the refugee. He thought, Hetty's on the warpath again!

* * *

As Ben had left, mulling over what he'd overheard, he spotted Sean in the street outside, wearing his ARP armband over his raincoat, a knapsack slung over the handlebars of his bike. Ben, his heart sinking, tried to stroll past casually, but Sean enquired loudly, 'What were you up to in there? Dad'll be hopping mad.'

To give himself time, Ben said, 'Where're you off to?'

'ARP exercises,' said Sean importantly. 'We've been drafted to help cut turf up in the bogs in the Dublin Mountains.' He got on his bike. 'Granny made me sandwiches and I took some of your comics, *Magnet* and *Gem*. We're meeting up the Ballyboden Road.'

If Ben could keep him talking Sean might forget what he'd seen. 'How long for? What about work?'

'I've a week's leave,' said Sean shortly, 'and you'd better tell me what *you're* up to.'

Even though Dad, after his most recent visit to the sanatorium, had seemed sadder but also a little softer and kinder, Ben knew he'd be in real trouble if Sean revealed that he was working for the Goldens.

'Spit it out, Specky,' jeered Sean. 'You look like a fish on a hook.'

Reluctant and fearful, Ben gabbled out the story – the cost of the broken window, the job as *Shabbos goy*, the money to help Mam ...

At first Sean, astonished, said, 'C'mon, you're coddin' me!' And to Ben's surprise, his brother, for a moment, looked at him in a different way, almost with – could it be respect?

Sean said defensively, '*I* give me wages to Granny – some of that's for Mam too, y'know.' He added, curious, jerking his head towards Number 17, 'Anyways, what's it like in there? I mean, do they talk to you?'

'Sometimes,' said Ben, not wanting to say too much. 'But they're mostly out.' He paused, 'They're just ordinary, like us.' He went on, 'Listen, Sean, don't tell Dad, he'll be raging.'

'That depends,' Sean drawled, adding casually, 'you hear anything in there about refugees?' When Ben hesitated he said threateningly, 'You'd better come clean.'

'Er, I heard something about a refugee on the run,' Ben mumbled, 'like they were saying at Uncle Matt's that night. But it's just some girl, she couldn't be–'

Puffing himself up like a turkey, Sean recited what he'd been instructed: 'Anyone – girls, women, and oul' ones – can be spies. The British want to occupy our ports, and the Germans might invade us to get to Britain.' He paused for effect. 'They told us anyone illegal *must* be reported.'

He started to pedal off. 'Anyways, I'm off,' he said in his normal voice. 'You'd better tell what you heard to the Guards before I get back or ...' He left the rest unsaid.

Ben's heart sank. He was in another mess, this time more serious. Surely it wasn't right to report a private conversation he wasn't meant to hear? Still, there'd been lots of warnings about spies and invasions, and Dad ... In the distance he spotted Smiler on his way up to call for him, and he could hear from the shouts that a game was starting down the street.

He watched Sean zip off as Smiler approached.

Ben felt a knot in his stomach. Now, what was he going to do?

* * *

On Monday after school Ben's mind was in a ferment. At the football game yesterday he'd played badly enough to be jeered. And this morning in school he nearly got a belting in Irish class for staring out the window at the slanting rain and missing his turn to read about the heroic deeds of the High King Brian Boru. Had Brian Boru ever been trapped by his own lies, like himself?

He knew there were black lies – the serious ones – and white lies, or fibs. His lies were meant to pay his share for the window, help Mam and avoid Dad's rage. Did they count as black or white?

He recalled how sometimes, when he or Sean were in trouble, Granny said warningly, 'Oh what a tangled web we weave, when first we practise to deceive.' Well, he was in a tangled web now, or more like a juggler, trying to keep several balls in the air. If Mam were home, she might give out, but she'd help sort it all out for him.

Maybe he could talk to Granny? But recently Ben had noticed how she'd become slower, her pallid face showing her weariness. He couldn't worry her now.

Dragging his feet miserably he approached the Garda Station in Kevin Street, wishing something would happen to prevent him going in. Having to give this information made him feel queasy. If they knew, it would anger the Goldens – especially Hetty – and, of course, endanger the girl on the run, whoever she was.

As he loitered outside trying to summon up courage, a familiar, confident voice – like the answer to a prayer – said, 'Ben, lad, you look as if you've got the weight of the world on your shoulders!'

It was Uncle Matt, passing by on his bike in his knitted hat, clay pipe in his mouth, and a cheerful grin.

Ben had never been so happy to see anyone. 'Now, young fella,' said Uncle Matt. 'Why're you hanging about here? Get on the back carrier and come home with me.'

As he slowly pedalled off, he told Ben, 'We got a letter from Paddy. Can't say where exactly he is, but at least he's all right.' Then, over his shoulder, he called, 'The good news is, there's a bit of your auntie's apple tart left.'

* * *

After a hug from Auntie Bridie and a mug of lemonade and a wedge of tart, Ben felt better. Upstairs, against the background of birds swooping and fluttering around the room, Ben, knowing that more lies would not help, told Uncle Matt the whole story. It was an enormous relief, as though he'd shed a heavy load that had weighed him down.

Uncle Matt sucked on his pipe for a while. 'Well, Ben, it's a mess, but I can see how you got into it. I'll not go into your father's part – he has some peculiar opinions – but there's a lot on his mind just now. And I must say that the oul' man Golden's a good man, helping you pay for the window, and not just throwing you a hand-out either.' He gently caressed a tiny golden canary, singing its heart out. Then he put a comforting hand on Ben's shoulder. 'My advice is for you to go home and forget about report-ing that poor girl.'

'But Sean–' Ben's voice shook.

'Leave young Sean to me. He's a bit full of himself these days. I'll talk sense into him.' He added sadly, 'It's what your mam would do.'

Then, briefly but graphically he explained to Ben the

reality of the Nazi threat. Ben knew that Matt had friends abroad who had fought with him in the Spanish Civil War who sent him British and American newspapers and reports. Ben often read them to him, but he didn't always understand the details.

'Our country's in danger, not just from a few spies, and certainly not from innocent refugees like that young girl, but from the evil of Hitler and the Nazis,' said Uncle Matt.

Ben was shocked to learn that if Ireland *were* invaded, all Jews, including neighbours like the Goldens and the Woolfsons, would be arrested, beaten, their homes and possessions confiscated, and they'd almost certainly be sent to prison camps in Europe where they would be horrifically treated and many would die. Matt told Ben that in Nazi-occupied countries, even trade unionists such as Matt himself, as well as gypsies and handicapped people were all being rounded up. 'Lots of people don't believe it,' said Matt, 'but it's happening.'

As he digested this, Ben murmured, 'I didn't realise ... I mean, I know you think we should be in the war against the Nazis, along with Paddy, but–'

'There's different views on that in this country,' Uncle Matt replied slowly, 'for reasons of history.' Dusk was falling as he put cloths over the bird cages for the night. As they went downstairs he added, 'But at least we can do our best to help the innocent victims when we get the chance. Anyway, immigrants bring new skills, new energy. We could do with that.'

Downstairs Auntie Bridie interrupted. 'Matt, you'd better let Ben get home for his tea.' She gave him a hug, and he breathed in her scent, reminding him for a moment of Mam.

Uncle Matt pointed to a sack by the front door. 'If you want to earn an extra few pence for your Mam you can call round tomorrow with your pal and bring the empties back to the pub,' he said. He winked. 'My poor oul' leg isn't up to it.'

On the way home Ben felt better, though he was still in a muddle about the Goldens. He resolved, on his next visit to the sanatorium, to talk it all over with Mam before the inevitable day when Dad found out that his son was a *Shabbos goy.*

11

The Dalkey Adventure

Hetty and Eddie waited at Nelson's Pillar in O'Connell Street for the Dalkey tram, in high spirits despite the blustery wind and nasty shower of rain. They'd brought Mossy and Flossy, both yapping excitedly. Aunt Millie, pleased they were having an outing, had donated their fares; and Hetty's ma had made sandwiches and invited Eddie back for supper.

Across the road loomed the General Post Office, its great stone pillars still pockmarked, as they knew from history lessons, by bullets from the 1916 Easter Rising.

'It's nice to get away,' said Hetty in heartfelt tones after a morning during which she had to listen to an excited Mabel recounting how wonderful the hop had been, how she and Michael had danced three foxtrots and that her feet were killing her. Her offer to show Hetty the steps was firmly refused.

'I just hope *I* never have to go to a hop,' Hetty told Eddie as they waited for the tram. 'If I did, you're probably the only boy who'd go with me.'

'It's not much fun going with your cousin,' he grinned, 'especially one who can't even dance.' They both looked down at the heavy iron frame on his leg.

'Well, I can't dance either, so that would suit me,' said Hetty.

'Anyway, I'll be in long trousers soon, after my Barmitzvah,' he said cheerfully. 'Then people won't notice my leg.'

The Number 8 tram rolled into the terminus along shining tracks set in the cobbles, the electric trolley wire above flashing vivid sparks. As the passengers disembarked, the driver walked down the centre aisle banging the seats back to face the other way, ending up at the far end, while the conductor raced up the stairs to wind the handle changing the destination from Nelson's Pillar to Dalkey.

'Oh good,' said Hetty excitedly. 'It's one of the balcony trams.'

The small knot of people waiting in the rain surged forward and climbed on. The conductor took their fares and punched the tickets.

'I see youse brought yer oul' guard dogs,' he grinned, patting the puppies. Then he swiped the bell and the tram rattled off.

Hetty and Eddie stood in the balcony – the open front of the upper deck – watching the city buildings give way to soft green countryside, hedgerows and cottage gardens sprinkled here and there with delicate snowdrops and golden crocuses. The rain stopped, and a watery sun appeared.

Familiar with the journey from Sunday afternoon outings with Zaida and Bobba, Hetty loved the moment when the tram reached Sydney Parade and she first caught sight of the sea, greeny-grey today, the surging waves capped with creamy foam.

The tram clattered past the elegant church in the middle of the road at Monkstown, through Dun Laoghaire – which older people always called 'Kingstown' – past the shops and the People's Gardens, and on into Dalkey village, bathed in Sunday peace.

They got off at the terminus beside the ancient castle. Eddie, glancing up at the clock said, 'It's early – we'll take the dogs for a walk first.' They were both nervous, but neither admitted it.

They set off down Castle Street with the two excited puppies on string leads, and turned left into Coliemore Road, catching glimpses of pink-washed stucco villas and graceful Georgian houses, with flights of steps up to the front door, behind wrought iron gates ornamented with weathered stone lions. Eventually they reached tiny Coliemore harbour, empty except for a few wooden rowboats used for fishing and a single sailing yacht.

'It's like a place from a fairy story,' exclaimed Hetty as they were dragged, laughing, down the flagstoned slipway by Mossy and Flossy, who then, finally given their freedom, rushed about, slipping on the rocks and investigating interesting new smells on the sandy shore.

Breathing in the fresh, salty air, Hetty and Eddie gazed across the sound to Dalkey Island with its mysterious, circular Martello tower, beyond it the Kish lighthouse, with Howth on the far side of the bay. Further out lay the open sea.

Eddie produced a KitKat, handing half to Hetty. 'Nothing between us and Britain–'

'And the war,' finished Hetty. Reminded of their task, Eddie produced a scrap of paper.

'St Patrick's Square,' he read out. 'Must be back in the village.'

With some difficulty they found the square of sturdy cottages surrounding a grassy green. Hetty lifted the brass knocker, shaped like a hand. Lace curtains twitched, and after a few moments an unsmiling woman in an apron opened the door. 'Yes?'

Hetty took a deep breath. 'We're ... er ... looking for a girl ... from Germany, who's staying here ... at least we think ...'

There was a silence. Then the woman said abruptly: 'She's gone. She paid off her rent and left yesterday.'

Disappointment washed over Hetty. 'I live at 17 Martin Street – maybe you could let her know?'

The woman looked suspicious.

'We're friends, we just want to help,' Eddie tried to

sound reassuring. 'D'you happen to know where she is?' The woman shook her head. Behind her a tall, heavy man in a white shirt and black trousers with braces appeared. 'Who is it?'

'Someone looking for Renata,' muttered the woman. Flossy let out a low growl, but Hetty and Eddie barely heard. Their eyes were on the jacket the man was pulling on.

It was a police uniform.

* * *

Baffled and weary, they sat on the homeward tram eating their sandwiches, with Mossy and Flossy, equally tired, curled cosily on their laps.

'I bet that Guard gave her away,' snorted Hetty.

'I don't think so,' said Eddie. 'Funny though, the way Flossy growled at him.'

'Mossy didn't, though. He's hopeless as a guard dog, he loves everybody.'

'If she'd been caught, we'd have heard,' Eddie persisted. 'But why was she staying in their house?' He frowned. 'It's odd the way that woman said her name, Renata, as though she was a friend.'

'It's not fair,' protested Hetty fiercely. 'You'd think she'd be let stay here. She's just a girl.' She stroked the puppy, a warm, comforting bundle.

'At least you left your address,' said Eddie, 'in case she goes back there.'

'Did your Da know anything else about her?'

Eddie thought hard. 'Something about her father having worked here, somewhere in the west of Ireland.' He sighed. 'I don't much like going behind Da's back.'

'He'd forgive you if we found her.'

He couldn't help smiling. 'Hetty, you're a born rescuer. First the puppies, now refugees–'

'The puppies mattered,' she insisted, 'but this time it's even more important. It's not a puppy, but a person.' The rabbi's words that had made such an impression on her, rose up in her mind: If I am for myself alone, what am I? And if not now, when?

And unexpectedly, she felt a wave of regret at the memory of Ben helping with that other rescue long ago. If only things were different and he could help now. But that was out of the question. A worrying thought struck her. 'You don't think he ... er ... Ben overheard us that day and told?'

Eddie looked troubled. 'I'm sure he wouldn't–' He broke off as they reached Nelson's Pillar. But now a troubling worm of suspicion was added to the complex mix of feelings Hetty had about Ben.

When they got off the Number 14 tram from the Pillar to Portobello bridge, it was much colder and almost dark, the street lamps creating soft pools of light as Hetty and Ben skirted the squat shapes of the barges moored in Portobello Harbour, past the Ever Ready battery factory, and home to Martin Street.

12

The Bombing

Hardly anyone heard the first warning sound in the early hours of the January morning – like the faint buzzing of an angry mosquito. Even the LDF recruits, including Ben's father, meant to be watching out at their depots around the city and in the Dublin mountains, noticed nothing.

In Martin Street, Hetty was roused from sleep by the insistent drumming of an aeroplane engine, at first distant, then louder. Not waiting for Mabel she pulled on a skirt and jumper, threw on her coat, and raced downstairs and out into the street. Flares lit up the sky as brightly as daylight, and the throbbing grew more powerful, culminating in a series of huge, reverberating, sickening crashes. Neighbours began to trickle out of their houses.

Hetty gazed at the sky and sped back upstairs. 'Quick, Da, come down!' she shouted. 'There's some kind of explosion. I think it's from the direction of Greenville Hall Synagogue!'

A few minutes later Leon Golden, hastily dressed, emerged and took one look at the thick plumes of smoke appearing above the rooftops. 'Looks like it's near Donore Avenue,' he gasped. 'Please God, Sam and Millie and Eddie are all right.' Motioning Mabel to stay with her mother and Solly, he set off at a run, with Hetty beside him.

As they left, Sean and Ben Byrne appeared. In the street there was a babble of talk. Neighbours, half-dressed, were asking each other if it was a bomb, and where it was. No one could believe neutral Ireland had been bombed by Nazi German warplanes.

'Bound to be the British,' said a neighbour who'd fought against Britain in the War of Independence and tended to think they were to blame for everything since.

When Ben saw that Sean, complete with armband, was setting off in a state of high excitement, he acted fast and jumped on the back of Sean's bike, clinging on to him as they swerved across the tramlines down the South Circular Road in the direction of Dolphin's Barn where clouds of smoke and dust billowed in the beams of the search-lights roaming the sky.

* * *

Although the destruction at Donore Avenue couldn't be compared to the huge raids on London, Belfast and other cities that they'd heard about, nevertheless, what both Hetty and Ben saw when, separately, they reached the scene, stayed with them all their lives.

On both sides of the street the trim houses with their neat gardens were wrecked. Roofs and chimneys were torn off, all windows smashed, huge slabs of concrete, bricks, shards of glass, roof tiles, twisted railings, broken furniture, even clothes and blankets lay around the street as if scattered by a giant hand.

At the heart of this chaotic scene there was an eerie silence. People walked in a daze, calling out names of loved ones or aimlessly picking up objects from the shambles; some sat or lay on the ground, while water gushed unheeded from broken mains. In the middle of the street the huge hole where three houses had stood was like the cavity left after teeth had been pulled from a familiar mouth. The air, full of dust and ash, was suffused with a strong smell of gas.

Amid the frantic activity of arriving police, soldiers, ARP, LDF, firemen directing hoses and ambulance men, Hetty stood hypnotised, staring at the gap where her aunt and uncle's house had been. Her father was already helping rescue workers digging feverishly in the rubble by torchlight, some with shovels, others with their bare hands.

Someone asked, 'Hetty, have you a relation here?' When she tried to answer, only a whisper came out. 'My aunt and uncle and my cousin.' She nodded towards the gap. 'That's ... that was their house.'

'They've got some people out,' a boy with an ARP armband muttered to her. 'They're down there, waiting for ambulances.'

Setting off to where he pointed, she noticed him joining the diggers and realised who he was – the older Byrne
brother from next door who'd returned Ma's cake. And
squinting, she realised that digging alongside him was
Ben.

Anxiously scanning everyone she met, Hetty hurried
down the road to where ambulances were arriving. And
to her enormous relief, Eddie appeared, white with dust,
limping towards her like a vision. With a cry she hurled
herself at him, nearly knocking him over. He rested his
head on her shoulder for a moment and whispered, 'Ma,
Da, are they all right?'

'They're digging them out,' she said reassuringly,
hoping against hope it was true. Then she heard a familiar
yapping. Glancing down she saw at Eddie's heels, Flossy,
whom the dust had turned into a pure white puppy – and
to her horror, Hetty burst into tears.

* * *

Afterwards Hetty recalled the scene in irregular snatches,
like a confused dream. She and Eddie tried to help dig,
but the chunks of masonry were too heavy for them. Now
and again there was a shout when a person was uncov-
ered or someone heard calling or groaning from under
the rubble.

More people arrived. One of them, an older man,

balding and thickset, wearing a woolly hat, seemed to know the Byrnes and immediately set to work beside them.

Watching with Eddie, Hetty noticed the easy strength of the older brother as he swung his shovel, and the younger boy's laboured breathing. Neighbours from the streets around appeared with flasks of hot tea and hastily-made sandwiches.

After what seemed like hours, Da called Hetty and Eddie over. He was smiling through the sweat and grime on his face. There, in a crater, still lying on their bed across which rested a heavy beam, which had, amazingly, protected them, she saw her aunt, clutching her shoulder in pain, and her uncle, both coated with dust and looking like ghosts, but alive.

They were lifted carefully on to stretchers. Uncle Sam managed to smile shakily as Eddie bent to give him a hug. Hetty felt relief welling up. As an ambulance drove up, the older man with the Byrne boys approached them.

'I believe you're neighbours of my nephews here, Sean and Ben?' he said to Da. 'I just want to say I'm glad your family's all right.'

Da shook his hand and said quietly, 'Many thanks to you – to all of you – for your help.' He turned to Hetty. 'Hetty, I'm going with them to Vincent's hospital. You go home with Eddie and tell Ma to have hot food ready. I'll bring them home as soon as they're released.' Then he added, 'Mabel should go to Zaida and Bobba before someone tells them the news and they start thinking the worst.'

* * *

Much later, Da returned with the news that Aunt Millie had been kept in hospital with a broken collar bone. Mabel had reassured Bobba and Zaida. Eddie and Uncle Sam, shocked and bruised but otherwise unhurt, slept on mattresses in the Goldens' parlour, with Flossy, who'd got a warm welcome from Mossy, curled up beside them.

For what was left of that night, once an over-excited Mabel had finally stopped talking, Hetty tossed and turned, images of the devastated street and Eddie limping towards her all whirling through her mind.

She also recalled Ben and Sean digging frantically with their uncle and so many others, concerned only for the trapped and injured. All on the same side. And yet she'd once vowed passionately never to speak to the Byrnes. How one dramatic night had changed everything!

Eventually she dropped into an uneasy sleep, to be woken only an hour or two later – like Ben next door – by the familiar clip clop of the milkman's horse and the chink of bottles on the doorstep, just as though every-thing was normal and nothing unusual had happened.

* * *

After an early breakfast, Hetty and Mabel, leaving Eddie still asleep, accompanied their father and uncle to salvage what they could from Donore Avenue. Zaida insisted on going with them, linked on either side by Uncle Sam and Mabel.

In the cold morning light the wrecked street, with police and ARP officers still on duty, resembled a battlefield.

Zaida gazed at the destruction. With the skullcap on his silver hair and lines of sorrow etched on his face he looked like an Old Testament prophet, and people glanced at him with sympathy.

No sign of Ben, but his uncle, who was still there helping out, came over and asked about Aunt Millie.

'She's in pain,' said Uncle Sam, 'but she'll be all right.' He touched his bruised forehead. 'We had a lucky escape.'

'It reminds us of what the war's really about,' Uncle Matt said earnestly to Zaida. 'You, sir, understand that better than us.' He paused. 'We're a bit smug here in Ireland, sheltering behind our neutrality.'

'Thanks again for your help,' said Uncle Sam.

At home Zaida sank into the armchair, his face still clouded. Uncle Sam put his arm round him. 'At least we're all safe, Papa, and Millie will be all right.'

'Amazing no one was killed in the raid,' said Da, 'except a parrot in a cage!'

'Poor parrot,' put in Hetty.

'But people are hurt,' said Zaida, 'and some have lost everything. And the synagogue–'

'The rabbi said the windows were smashed, but the holy scrolls are unharmed,' Da reassured him. 'There's debris and dust, but the lights are working.'

'And the Presbyterian church isn't badly damaged either,' put in Mabel. 'That's where my friend Alison goes.'

As they sat over cups of tea, Zaida muttered, 'The destruction, the violence, they remind me ...' His voice tailed off.

'Abbie, it's not a pogrom,' said Bobba briskly. 'It's not persecution like we had in the *heim* – our old home. That would only happen here if the Nazis came.'

'I know,' mumbled Zaida. 'But still ...'

Hetty picked up Solly and plonked him on Zaida's lap. The child reached up to Zaida's bristly cheek, and Zaida was soon jigging him on his knee while Solly crowed with joy and blew bubbles.

There were approving nods and smiles from the grown-ups, which, Hetty reflected, didn't come her way very often.

13

Money Troubles

In the next few weeks, the immediate excitement of the bombing died down, the houses were being rebuilt, and Aunt Millie was recovering. But Hetty couldn't get the plight of the refugee, Renata, out of her head. Every day she waited in vain to see if there was a letter or message from her. She and Eddie had decided to say nothing until they'd actually made contact with her, so Hetty was trying to act normally. Not that that was difficult, as everyone's mind was on different matters.

First there had been a argument at home after her father had slipped off to Powers at Kelly's Corner to 'put a few bob on the gee-gees'. It appeared his horse had won and he got the few bob all right, but then lost it all again backing another 'dead cert'.

The atmosphere in the house was tense. Ma was very cross and worried. But fortunately, that evening Carmel and Maureen came to show off their outfits for the Irish step dancing competition in the Rotunda Winter Gardens. Everyone admired the dresses and sashes in scarlet, green and gold, with braid and tassels, made by their auntie from oddments of material.

'Show us a bit of a dance,' begged Mabel, and they did,

arms straight by their sides, feet tapping and twinkling and their identical red curls bouncing. Even Hetty watched admiringly, and Da came downstairs to have a look and managed a weak smile. When the girls had gone, Mabel complained, 'Why can't *we* do Irish dancing?'

'Or tap dancing?' Hetty put in.

'Yeah!' agreed Mabel. 'You wear lovely shiny shoes with metal studs and bows. I saw Fred Astaire and Ginger Rogers doing it in a film, they were so fast–'

But Ma, her usually cheerful face grim, snapped, 'There's no money for any of that nonsense.' She looked pointedly at Da, who grabbed the *Evening Mail* and crept back upstairs.

Mabel said eagerly, 'I could leave school and work in a shop–' She stopped short. 'Though I s'pose Michael mightn't like it!'

'Oh really, Mabel,' Hetty burst out, 'who cares what a snob like him thinks? Is he going to help us out when the rent's due?'

'You're just jealous,' protested Mabel, 'because you haven't got a boyfriend–'

'No, and I don't want one,' spat Hetty, 'at least not if he's like your precious Michael–'

'Girls, please,' said Ma wearily, as Mabel rushed upstairs and slammed the bedroom door behind her. 'This isn't a time for quarrels.'

Hetty scooped Mossy into her arms and cuddled him. I'm the only one who talks straight in this house, she thought.

And now she wouldn't be able to get into the bedroom to do her homework or read the latest *School Friend* comic, donated by Mabel's friend Alison, for at least half an hour.

* * *

A week later, without warning, the blow fell. Da came home late, looking troubled. Ma had just finished sweeping the kitchen floor and handed Mabel the tin of Cardinal red polish and a rag.

'Well, Leon?' Ma asked him in a resigned tone. '*Now* what's wrong?'

'Not the "gee-gees" again!' Hetty whispered to Mabel.

After a long pause, he muttered, 'A wage cut.'

'Oy!' Ma's rosy face turned pale.

'It could be worse,' said Da quickly. 'I could have been sacked. They're cutting back on the bespoke suits, and there's a new machine that does buttonholes–'

'But the rent?' Ma's anxious tones echoed Mabel's and Hetty's thoughts. 'And we owe some of the shops as it is.'

'It'll be all right.' He forced a cheerful tone. 'The Lord will provide.' Putting on his coat he announced, 'I'm going to prayers, we'll talk later.'

As the door slammed, Ma sank down at the table, her head in her hands. She was always the strong person in the house through thick and thin, and the girls had never seen her so shattered. Mossy, sensing the atmosphere, gave a little whine.

Even Hetty was perturbed. 'Will I make you a cup of tea?' she asked Ma.

In a low voice, almost as if talking to herself, Ma said, 'It's not only the rent, shoes and clothes, it's the other things, like food. The traditions, the hospitality, the nurturing are part of our life, of who we are, of who *I* am ...' her voice broke. '*Now* we could do with the savings.' Knowing where the savings had gone, they were silent.

Mabel jumped up. 'That's it!' she declared. 'I'm going to leave school and get a job.' Her mother tried to interrupt, but she carried on, 'Carmel's cousin got a job in the Monument Creamery in Rathmines. She says it's not bad, you get a little white apron and hat, and leftover butter and eggs at the end of the day. I could help with the rent and,' she paused, a dreamy look in her eyes, 'maybe there'll even be enough to perm my hair, like Alison.'

Hetty snorted, recalling the perm, which had made Alison look as if she'd been electrocuted.

Sipping the tea, Ma began to perk up. 'You're not to leave school, Mabel,' she declared. 'There's your future to consider. I can do dressmaking and alterations, that'll help. We'll manage somehow,' she said, more like her usual brisk self. 'If the worst comes to the worst, at least you could be trained in typing or tailoring. That's better than a shop.'

'But I can always go to night school later,' pleaded Mabel. 'In the Monument I'd be earning straight away.'

'Not much,' retorted Ma.

'I could get a job after school,' put in Hetty.

'Nonsense!' snapped Ma, 'you'll be needed to help me here.'

A roar from upstairs announced that Solly was awake, and normal life, for the moment, took over.

* * *

Hetty thought she'd never get through that week. Whatever about Da's occasional gambling, a wage cut was a bad blow. Even though he snapped at her sometimes, she felt sorry for him. This wasn't his fault, and it was happening to others too. At least he hadn't lost his job.

But there was a deep sense of insecurity in the house, and endless arguments about Mabel's future. Hetty herself remained in a permanent bad temper at being expected to do more than her share of chores while this went on. The only good thing was that a second-hand pram had been passed on to them by a friend of Aunt

Millie's, so she could now take Solly for walks and escape from the house.

She wondered if Ben knew about her da. Maybe he'd have to stop working for them, though it was Zaida who left his weekly payment. That would mean she'd never see him. She felt an unexpected jolt of disappointment at the thought.

But what bothered her even more, like an itch nothing would soothe, was that there was still no word from Renata.

Two days later, when Hetty arrived home from school, the house was unusually empty. Mabel had gone to Alison's and Ma had taken Solly with her to buy material for a skirt for her first customer, a neighbour of Bobba's.

In the hall, she stooped to pick up a torn piece of paper which had been pushed through the letterbox. There was no name, but she unfolded it, her heart thumping.

At that moment Ma came back with Solly and a parcel of material. Noticing the paper she asked, 'What's that?'

'Nothing,' said Hetty. Quickly she pulled her coat back on. 'Just going round to Eddie's.' And she sped off, the folded note clutched in her hand.

* * *

Luckily Eddie was alone in his house, working on an intricate balsa-wood model of a Spitfire fighter plane. He listened as Hetty read the note, in strange, foreign-looking, loopy handwriting:

Liebe Hettie!

My englisch not good.

I came you house by address I got from family at Dalkey. I need help, my visa not good, I must to meine Papa go in other part Irland. I try come again but I must be carefully, not to be sent away.

Renata Stern.

'No address,' Hetty groaned. 'If only I'd got back earlier!'

'Let's hope no one noticed her,' said Eddie worriedly. 'Maybe she'll come again.' He rose. 'Nothing we can do now. Want to stay for a bit, maybe have a game of draughts? I've done my homework.'

'Well, I haven't touched mine, and anyway there's trouble at home.'

'I heard,' said Eddie sympathetically.

'Zaida offered to help,' said Hetty, 'and your da, too. But still …'

'It'll be all right, Hetty.' Eddie patted her shoulder. 'And Zaida said he wants to go on paying Ben, so at least that won't change.'

One positive thing on this black day, reflected Hetty as

she set off home, though she wasn't sure why Ben's job continuing made her feel better. Strange, too, that despite the money problems piling up at home, she felt somehow that saving Renata would make it easier to tackle everything else.

14

Echoes of the Past

But someone *had* noticed the foreign girl dropping the note.

Ben had been watching for the glimmer man again. It was spilling rain but at least that meant there was no football game to torment him. He'd picked up hints about the wage cut, and the Goldens' money troubles somehow showed they were just like everyone else, whatever Dad said about them.

But would it mean an end to his job? He'd just begun to get accustomed to the Golden household – to Mossy's welcome, Zaida's jokes and stories, the spicy smell of Mrs Golden's 'kuchen' cake, baked on Fridays for the Sabbath, a piece always left out for him on the table.

Even Hetty had thawed slightly. Last week she'd brought down Solly, in a blue jacket knitted by Bobba. As she strapped him into the bulky old pram with its huge wheels, strong black hood for rain and green-fringed sunshade, Solly gave Ben an amiable, dribbly smile showing two tiny teeth. Ben made clicking noises with his tongue and smiled back, and so, for a moment, did Hetty.

But what would she say, an insistent voice in his head whispered, if she knew he'd once nearly reported the refugee she was trying so hard to save?

As his thoughts circled, he took care to keep an eye out for the glimmer man. So he was quick to notice a strange girl walking down the street, peering at the house numbers. She was tall and thin, an ill-fitting check jacket pulled tightly around her and a headscarf tied over her bright hair.

As she knocked hesitantly at Number 17, Ben wondered at first if she was some friend or relation of the Goldens. She knocked again, and in that instant he realised who she must be – the famous refugee whom everyone was searching for! The girl whose name he didn't know, whom he had almost betrayed.

Certain it was her, he jumped to his feet. Then he stopped. If he went down to talk to her, she'd probably take fright and run away. And anyway, what would he say? And Dad was due home from work soon and might spot them both. That would be a disaster.

Thanks to the rain the street was empty. He watched her take a scrap of paper and pencil from her bag, scribble a note and drop it through the letter-box. Then she left.

Although Ben had barely glimpsed her face, all the talk and discussion and simplistic labels faded away and she suddenly became not a possible spy, not even just a refugee, but a real girl, a vulnerable girl, a girl in trouble.

* * *

The following Saturday Ben arrived early at Number 17, wondering if they'd got the note from the girl. Hetty, putting the breakfast dishes in the sink, barely greeted him. Later, when she brought Solly down – smiling and pointing at Ben with his chubby little hand – Zaida had arrived and invited Ben into the parlour to identify for him, as he'd promised to do ever since he found Ben gazing at them, the people in the sepia photographs on the wall.

'That was my father, may he rest in peace,' Zaida said, indicating the white-bearded, hawkfaced old man whom Ben had noticed. 'He passed away after I left home. That's my mother beside him holding the youngest grandchild, and my sisters and their families.' He gazed unseeingly out of the window at the street. 'The last time I saw my father was in the field near our home in Lithuania, in a *shtetl* – a village called Akmiyan, a long way from here. I had learned some tailoring there from my father.' He gave Ben a sad smile. 'I was pulling up beets and he came out to warn me – Cossack soldiers were raiding the *shtetl*, there were screams and smoke and flames …' He paused, his voice husky. 'My father said, "They're rounding up young men for the Tsar's army. You must leave *now*, my son."'

Zaida turned to Ben who'd listened politely at first, but was now transfixed. 'Young men had to do twenty-five years' military service – and very few Jews ever came home after it. I had no money or papers – I was only wearing a ragged shirt.' He looked down at his Sabbath suit. 'My father took off his greatcoat, put it over my shoulders, gave me a few kopeks and a loaf of rye bread, and told me to go to my oldest sister, Mariashe.' He gave a bitter smile. 'I'd never even seen her. She left home for England before I was born.'

Hetty stood listening, though she must have heard it all before. But Ben was staggered. 'How did you manage with no money?' he asked. 'Did the soldiers catch up with you?'

Sinking into the easy chair, Zaida told Ben about the long, difficult journey to England, taking over a year, and from there later to Ireland. Along the way his tailoring skills earned him a little money, and he also did farm work, often sleeping in haybarns with the animals.

During Zaida's story, when his English failed him, he had to put in the odd Yiddish word. Zaida was still recounting it when Mr Golden descended the stairs. 'Come, Papa,' he said gently, 'it's time for the service.'

Zaida looked round vaguely, as though he had just returned from a journey and wasn't sure where he was. As his son took his arm, he said uncertainly, 'Of course, we mustn't be late for the synagogue.' He smiled at Ben regretfully. 'I'll tell you more, young man, another time.'

Putting on his worn greatcoat he added: 'This coat – it's the one my father gave me. He made it himself.'

As they left, Ben drew a deep breath: so that's how people became refugees. He thought of the girl on the run. His eyes met Hetty's and he saw that her normally hostile expression had vanished, if only for a moment, and a kind of spark flamed between them, a newfound link, across the barriers that divided them.

15

The Barmitzvah

In the Golden household the battle about Mabel's future raged, while Da, when he was not at work or prayer, kept out of the way. Despite Mabel's scholarship to the secondary school, and even with help from Uncle Sam and a little from Zaida, money was still very tight, and the price of kosher food was going up, along with everything else.

One evening, a week before Eddie's Barmitzvah, Mabel told Hetty that Carmel and Maureen had offered to bring her to see their cousin Sadie at work in the Monument Creamery. At the time Mabel was lying prone on the bed, her face gleaming white as a ghost as she applied Pond's 7-day Cold Cream Beauty Treatment which Alison had given her, swearing it would do wonders for her skin.

'Er, Hetty,' she asked, barely moving her lips because of the cold cream, 'will you come with me? You could help me persuade Ma and Da to let me work there.'

Hetty, deep in her library book, *The Scarlet Pimpernel*, was taken aback. 'What about Michael, the medical student? Wouldn't he disapprove?'

'He needn't know,' said Mabel, adding bitterly, 'anyway, when he saw me at the tennis competition in Carlisle on

Sunday he didn't even come over, just threw me a sort of casual wave, like you'd throw a dog a bone.'

'I told you so,' said Hetty smugly. She turned a page. 'All right, I'll come if you promise not to go on about everyone's boyfriend.'

Mabel started to say, 'What else is there...?' but the cold cream had stiffened her face and she could barely move a muscle. Hetty sniggered as she went back to her book.

But the next day Mabel happened to call in to Carmel when her cousin, Sadie, was visiting. Asked about the Monument, she'd declared, 'The work's desperate, half-eight to six, on your feet all day, and the pay's no good.' Looking strained, she added, 'You get a bit of butter and a few eggs, but the manageress tells you off if you even chat for a minute.'

After that, Mabel muttered, 'Maybe I'll try the typing or the tailoring.'

* * *

Then, suddenly it seemed to Hetty, preoccupied with finding Renata and with thoughts of Ben, Eddie's Barmitz-vah was upon them, with the Passover festival coming up soon after.

Da found some overtime work, and Ma got busy alter-ing a frock of Mabel's for Hetty. It was an unbecoming shade of greyish brown satin called 'mole', and had puff sleeves. Ma added pearl buttons and a Peter Pan collar from Cassidy's 'to give it a lift', as she put it. To Hetty these additions made the dress even more revolting. Everyone, she complained, even Solly in his little blue baby suit, looked better than her.

But on the big day, in the Greenville Hall Synagogue – now repaired – everyone watched Eddie, in a white prayer cap embroidered with silver thread by Bobba, his new long trousers covering his leg-iron, recite the portion of the Talmud, the Holy Law, following the Hebrew words on the ancient parchment scroll with a long silver instrument shaped like a pointing finger. His Da and Zaida stood beaming beside him and even Hetty felt a swell of pride in her cousin.

At the celebration dance that evening in the synagogue hall everyone rushed to congratulate the family and wish them *Mazal tov*. Ma, Bobba and Aunt Millie sat in a row, dressed in their best. As the mother of the Barmitzvah boy, Aunt Millie wore a long lime-green satin dress and stylish matching hat. Beside them, Hetty frowned as the guests waltzed and fox-trotted to Minda Myers' band. Mabel sat miserably in her blue taffeta dress, having spent hours – on Alison's advice – applying Vaseline to her eyelashes and rinsing her hair three times in lemon juice and vinegar to make it shine before curling it. But despite it all, she was being ignored by Michael Simons.

Things brightened up when he finally strolled over to invite a blushing Mabel to dance, and Eddie, scrubbing his face with his handkerchief to remove the scarlet lip-sticked kisses planted on his cheeks by his joyful female relations, came to sit beside Hetty.

'Any news?' he asked quietly.

'No,' she hissed. 'We must do something.'

'Da says she's gone to ground. No one can find her.'

An obstinate look, well-known to Eddie, came over Hetty's face. '*We* will find her,' she whispered fiercely.

The music stopped and Michael Simons returned Mabel speedily to her seat, and then strode off without a word.

Hetty, furious, had her mouth open to make a rude remark about him when Bobba said sharply to Mabel, 'That young man is too full of himself.' She sniffed. 'You should find a nicer boy.'

Mabel, her head bent, burst into tears. 'But he's a medical student,' she wailed. Everyone fussed around, offering her glasses of water or Ciderette. As Mabel's friend, Rebecca, rushed over to comfort her, Bobba murmured approvingly to Hetty, 'I don't think *you'll* be taken in by someone like him!'

Zaida, sitting across the table, reached over to pat Mabel's cheek. 'Never mind that boychik,' he murmured

135

gently. 'What really matters is that we're all here on this solemn but happy day – and our Eddie has become a man!'

Hetty, catching Eddie's eye, managed to suppress a giggle as she whispered, 'Plus, our Eddie's getting sloppy kisses, lots of hugs and pats on the back, and' – she paused wickedly – 'presents.'

'Sorry to disappoint you,' Eddie whispered back, 'but the presents are mostly religious books, prayer shawls and a fountain pen. Not one model aeroplane!'

16

The Football Match

The spring of 1941 came late, but finally a froth of pink and white blossom appeared, gardens were filled with daffodils and then scarlet tulips, and in the early morning before the siren summoned workers to the factories and his father slammed the door on his way out, Ben could hear the sweet singing of sparrows and blackbirds.

His spirits rose. He'd got a job cleaning out a neighbour's yard, and another from the Goldens' Uncle Sam humping a wheelbarrow full of evil-smelling horse manure collected from the roadway for the potatoes in the front garden of his house. As Uncle Sam paid him, they surveyed the drooping plants. 'A fat lot of use these'll be for feeding us through the Emergency, even with the manure,' he sighed. 'But they've told us to grow food, so that's what I'm trying to do.'

Granny was in better form, and Dad paid a rare visit to Mam in Crooksling, though he went straight to the pub on his return and came back very late. A few days earlier Uncle Matt had told Ben that he'd discouraged Sean from reporting the refugee. 'I warned him to stay out of it,' he reassured Ben. 'I think he'll drop it now.'

Ben, however, knowing Sean as he did, had his doubts.

In fact, Ben had heard nothing more about the mysterious refugee and wondered had Hetty and Eddie been to Dalkey. What he couldn't forget was that stirring, wordless look between himself and Hetty at the end of Zaida's story. Did it mean they might become friends? That she'd trust him – though why should she? Or was it just a passing glance, meaning nothing? He'd never had a girl as a friend before and the idea excited him, though it scared him too.

* * *

The weather changed. On a gusty, showery Sunday afternoon Ben and Smiler were sitting on the windowsill of Number 19 looking through *William and ARP,* which Ben had borrowed from the library.

Nothing much was happening in the wet street, but then Sean appeared and said carelessly, 'Er, Billy's sick. We were goin' to see Rovers playing Shels at Milltown. Youse two want to come?' They didn't have to think twice. Ben rushed to get his raincoat, gave a shout upstairs to Granny, got two pence off Dad who was snoozing in the *súgán* chair, then, perched precariously on the crossbar, with Smiler on the back carrier, Sean zoomed off before anyone tried to stop them.

Bumping along, clutching tightly to the handlebars, Ben remembered Sundays in past years, when Dad used to take them to matches at Milltown. On the way home, weary and happy, Dad would crack jokes and they'd argue about the game – every goal, every penalty, every save.

In recent times, although Sean still went with his friends, somehow the heart had gone out of those matches for Ben, like so much since Mam had got sick. But now things were looking up. Soon Mam would be home, and Dad would cheer up and bring them again like he used to.

As they approached Glenmalure Park the crowd swelled to thousands, a sea of faces, mostly men and boys in caps and raincoats walking up towards the football ground. Hundreds of bikes were parked four-deep against the wall all along the road. They parked Sean's bike near a group of women with boards balanced on old prams and heaped with fruit, calling, 'Get yer apples, two fer a penny.'

The turnstile was jammed with people. None of the three of them had the necessary sixpence to get in, so they burrowed into the crowd of boys, all supposedly under fourteen and hoping to get in free, begging the adults, 'Gi'e us a lift.' Smiler, the smallest of the three, was obligingly hauled over the gate, leaving Sean and Ben in the crowd outside.

As Sean pleaded loudly, the man at the gate said, 'Will you go away out o' that, the last time you saw fourteen was on the back of a bus!' There was a roar of laughter, and the crush got thicker as people pushed from behind. Ben, separated from both Sean and Smiler, was about to give up and plod home, the chances of an exciting after-noon receding, when a familiar voice called his name. He whirled round to see Eddie Golden grinning at him, and behind him his father.

'Hey, you can come in the stand with us,' said Eddie. 'My Da's a member.'

Ben was flabbergasted. He knew Eddie supported Shamrock Rovers and sometimes went to matches, but he never thought they'd be members of the club. 'Er, well ...' he muttered, 'there's me brother, and Smiler ...'

'Fine,' said Uncle Sam, 'plenty of room.' Ben called Sean, then Uncle Sam showed his card, the attendant pressed the pedal to release the turnstile, and in a flash the boys were through.

Sean, recognising Uncle Sam and Eddie from the bombing, hesitated about going to the stand, and so did Ben. But Smiler joined them, and grinning from ear to ear hissed: 'C'mon! The stand, for free! What're we waiting for?'

* * *

In the stand, supporters of both sides were crowded to-gether on the terraces, music was playing, and, led by

Sean, the boys squeezed and wriggled their way close to the pitch. The Rovers players, in their distinctive white jerseys with green hoops, ran from the corner pavilion through a gap made by the crowd. A deafening cheer went up, and everyone shouted, 'C'mon on, Jimmy!', 'Go for it, Paddy.' The Shelbourne players followed, to a smaller cheer. This was Rovers' home ground after all.

Play was fast and furious, and as the referee blew his whistle for half-time, Ben, at his first match for a year, was in seventh heaven. The cheering, booing, insults and slagging were music to his ears. But Sean grumbled, 'No goals.'

'Still, great save by Larry Palmer,' replied Eddie, 'when he was at the edge of the box and the ball was lobbed over him and the other crowd all shouted "Goal!", but he got back and saved it!'

'Yeah,' agreed Sean, taken aback, Ben noticed, by Eddie's enthusiasm.

'Er, d'you play yerself?' Sean asked Eddie. Ben, realising that Eddie's leg-iron was hidden by his new long trousers, glanced at him anxiously. But Eddie said casually, 'I used to play, before' – he hesitated, looking down at his leg – 'before I got polio. I usually played in goal.' He grinned. 'I was never much good.' Sean stopped short at the mention of polio.

As play re-started the rain grew heavier, the pitch

muddier, the heavy leather ball more sodden, the players more weary – and still no goal. The crowd never tired, with cheers or catcalls for the players and torrents of abuse for the referee.

Frustration was starting to build up, suddenly defused by a shout of laughter from the players, the crowd and even the referee, when a Shels player ran flat out down the pitch chasing the ball – which he had no chance of catching – and a voice cried out, 'Open the gates!'

'Ten minutes to go,' called out a Shels supporter beside them. 'Better get a move on.'

'I was hoping for a bit more magic from Paddy Moore,' said Sean.

'Yeah, he's usually brilliant,' agreed Eddie. 'Easily the best centre forward in the league.'

'And what about Jimmy Dunne?' put in Smiler. 'He's played for Sheffield United, and Arsenal.'

'Well, neither of them's any use now,' said Sean. 'We must be mad standing out here, getting drenched, to watch this rubbish. Rovers are useless today!'

But Ben thought this was the best Sunday he'd had for ages. All his troubles had melted away – his mam, his dad, the Goldens, the refugee, even Hetty, in the magic of the game. He looked up for a moment at the dark clouds above moving to shut out a stray beam of sunshine. For some reason, a shiver ran through him.

And in the next instant Paddy Moore streaked through the defence, lashed a vicious shot and, as they collectively held their breaths, slammed in a glorious goal, right in front of their eyes.

The crowd went mad, Ben, Smiler, Sean and Eddie with them. Arms around each others' shoulders they sang, cheered and shouted till they were hoarse. Even the Shels supporters had to admire the skill of that goal.

They were all grinning when they rejoined Uncle Sam, and so was he. They said their farewells, and even Sean thanked him enthusiastically.

'It's the Passover festival next week,' Uncle Sam told them, 'but maybe we'll do this again before the season ends.' And shaking hands with all of them, he went off with Eddie.

They wobbled home on the bike, avoiding the tram tracks and puddles, reliving every detail of the match at the tops of their voices.

'Er, that uncle of theirs,' Sean jerked his head towards the Goldens' house as they turned into Martin Street, the setts gleaming from the rain, 'he's not a bad fella.' He grinned at Ben. 'All the same, better not tell Dad!' And Ben, relieved, grinned back.

As Sean slowly pedalled up the road with the others walking alongside, Ben noticed a figure outside their house. It was Dad, in his Sunday suit, which he usually changed out of after Mass, and he seemed to be waiting for them. It looked like something was wrong. Maybe he'd found out about Ben's job.

When they reached him, Ben saw that his face was sombre, and his eyes puffy and bloodshot. Instead of shouting at them, he said nothing, just cleared his throat and swallowed. A terrible fear spread through Ben.

Sean said, 'Dad, what is it, what's happened?'

Dad cleared his throat again.

Sean almost shouted, 'Dad!'

In a low voice, Dad said finally, 'It's – Mam.'

'Is she worse?' said Sean with increasing urgency. 'Has she taken a turn?'

'Your mam ...' Dad paused, and in that moment of silence Ben knew.

Mam had died, and he would never see her again.

17

My Mother Wore
a Yellow Dress

At the house a black-edged card had been pinned to the front door to tell neighbours the news. Granny, waiting inside, held the boys close, wordlessly.

Relations arrived – Uncle Matt, his eyes red, gripping Ben's and Sean's shoulders and saying over and over again, 'Poor lads, poor lads'; Auntie Bridie, bringing an enormous parcel of sandwiches and cake into the kitchen, kissing them, their faces made damp by her tears.

Then other people started calling to the house, with Auntie Bridie and Granny's friend Josie helping her to make tea. Many of the neighbours, both Christian and Jewish, left in food – and this time Dad made no protest.

Dad's face was grim and he said little, but later that evening he came into the boys' bedroom. Sean was asleep, but Ben lay awake, icy and shivering. Dad went downstairs and brought him up the stone hot-water bottle that Mam had used. 'Heated on the glimmer,' he whispered. Ben clutched it to him, relishing the comforting warmth, as Dad muttered, 'It's just ye lads and me now.

We have to help Granny. We have to go on without your mam–' His voice broke, and touching Ben's shoulder he left the room.

As the dreaded funeral approached, Dad's face grew more forbidding; the moment of warmth towards Ben had vanished. Granny, grief-stricken as she was, tried to comfort them all.

But Ben felt bitter and resentful. He couldn't believe Mam had left them, that she'd gone on a journey alone, with no chance to say goodbye. Anger welled up inside him, followed by more anger with himself for blaming her.

Granny reminded him it wasn't Mam's fault; this dreadful disease had struck so many, young and old. Consumption has no pity for blue eyes and golden hair, Ben recalled. Where was that girl now, seen once in the sanatorium? Same as his mam, he supposed, and it filled him with despair.

* * *

On the morning of the funeral Ben and Sean went to Uncle Matt's for their breakfast. No one spoke much. Sean shovelled in the generous fry Auntie Bridie dished up, but despite her pleas, Ben couldn't get anything past the heavy lump of grief, pain, fear, anger – whatever it was – stuck in his throat. Uncle Matt put his arm around him and brought him up to the room full of birdsong. He drew the curtains together and began to cover the birdcages.

'But it's morning,' Ben protested.

'It's a mark of respect,' his uncle said, 'for Marie.' And gradually in the darkened room the birds fell silent.

Then Uncle Matt called Sean upstairs, sat them both down and handed them an envelope. 'It's for the two of you,' he muttered. 'She gave it to me on my last visit.' He cleared his throat. 'She hadn't much strength to write.'

Together they read her words, in weak, wavery writing – saying how much she loved them both, how proud of them she was and would always be; that they were always to remember that Dad loved them too, even when he didn't show it; and finally, they were not to think of her as gone; she would still be watching over them, always there when they needed her, only they couldn't see her. Ben, fingering his conker for comfort, fought down the lump which threatened to turn to tears. Even tough, strong Sean was silent. But they felt consoled.

On the way downstairs Uncle Matt stopped and turned to Ben, just behind him. 'Remember what she said, Ben,' he whispered. 'Whatever you do, try to make her proud.'

The rest of the day passed in a blur – Ben and Sean in their Sunday suits walking slowly with Dad and Uncle Matt behind the sombre carriage drawn by four black-plumed horses. Behind them came Granny and Auntie Bridie, supported by a flood of relations, neighbours and family friends.

In Martin Street all the blinds were drawn. As they passed Number 17, Ben saw that the door was open and Mrs Golden and the girls, along with other Jewish neighbours, had joined the crowd on the roadside. Hetty, carrying Solly in her arms, was frowning as usual, but she stared at Ben, her attention totally focused, and, Ben felt, full of sympathy. Ben's heart lightened a little. At the top of the road Smiler, for once unsmiling, stood cap in hand with Billy, the Woolfsons and the rest of the football crowd, along with Carmel and Maureen and other girls from Martin Street, watching the funeral procession pass.

Ben kept his eyes averted from the coffin, almost hidden under bright wreaths and bunches of spring flowers. As Uncle Matt had said, better to think of her as she had been – slender, but not yet painfully thin, laughing in her butter-yellow dress with the white lace collar and big white buttons.

Afterwards the house was crowded again. People ate and drank, approaching the mourners to murmur above the babble of talk, 'Sorry for your trouble' … 'She was a grand lady'… 'So young.' The priest put a hand on the boys' shoulders, saying, 'The Lord giveth and the Lord taketh away …' A few people pressed sixpences into Ben's hand, and Ben realised he could finally pay off his window debt, but it was small comfort.

Finally Ben escaped upstairs. Passing the door of

Mam's room, he felt compelled to go in. The gas fire was unlit, the neatly made bed empty, tiny dust motes floated in the air and her scent still lingered.

Hearing footsteps on the stairs he hastily ran into his own room – mercifully empty – closed the door, flung himself on his bed, and for the first time since Mam's death cried in great gulping sobs until he thought his heart would break.

* * *

As the days passed Ben entered a long dark tunnel which seemed to have no ending. Soon after the funeral Dad had fallen into one of his bitter dark moods, and spent most evenings in the pub. They heard him returning late, shouting and crashing into the furniture, sometimes calling Mam's name.

Sean was back at work and out playing football every evening. 'Won't bring Mam back to be sitting around, missing the game,' he told Ben.

'He's right, Ben,' said Granny softly. But when Uncle Matt called around, he often found Granny herself half-dozing in the *súgán* chair, her gnarled little hands, usually so busy with knitting or darning or her rosary beads, inert on her lap. When neighbours called or the boys were home, she brightened a little.

Ben himself had no energy or enthusiasm for anything

– not even when Smiler challenged him to a game of marbles or conkers, or called to show him a new set of cigarette cards, Mysteries of the Microscope, he was collecting.

In school Ben did the minimum, and at home he decided to give up the job of *Shabbos goy*. What was the point in risking Dad's anger to earn extra money now? His debt had been paid off and after that it was all going to be for Mam. His growing interest in the Goldens, his concern for the refugee, even the fascination with Hetty had faded away now, and life seemed empty and hopeless.

* * *

A couple of weeks later, on Ben's return from school, Granny told him Mrs Golden had called to offer sympathy. She'd brought some matza crackers which she explained were customary at Passover, and she'd joked, 'Don't be sending them back, now!'

They'd had a cup of tea and a nice chat. Ben was pleased Granny was in better spirits. She'd even done some baking herself like she used to, and offered him a custard tart, one of his favourites. As he ate she told him, 'That lady spoke very well of *you*, pet.'

Apparently Mrs Golden had said, hesitantly, that the family understood Ben's grief, but when he was up to it, they hoped he might return to the job. 'Zaida – my father-in-law – is happy to pay his wage, though it's not much, I know. Having a fire on the Sabbath is such a help to us,' Mrs Golden had said. 'But also, we all miss him, even baby Solly and the puppy.'

That had made Granny smile, and Ben, hearing her words, felt a warmth, a tiny loosening of the knot of misery that accompanied him wherever he went. He wondered had Hetty missed him? He doubted it.

'That lady's right, like Sean is, pet. Life has to go on,' Granny said. 'I mind the time when my da passed on. I was thirteen, and we had to sell the farm and move to Dublin. There was no welfare then – not that there's much now.' As a young girl she'd had to work long hours in Judd's Hide and Skin Yard – 'you wouldn't believe the stink!' – and then in a brickworks in Dolphin's Barn pushing heavy wheelbarrows full of bricks which had been fired in the kilns. 'I'd be jaded,' she said, 'and then dashing home to help get the tea.' Then she smiled and added, 'But Sundays after Mass we still had fun with our pals.'

'Was Josie one of your pals?' asked Ben, glad to see her brighter.

'She was indeed, and we used to bring a picnic of bread and a bit of cheese for all us young ones, and cross the hump-backed bridge over the canal. The other side was open country and we'd roam around, picking wild flowers, climbing gates, chasing geese, though Josie was afraid of them.' She stopped with a wistful smile. 'We were young, we had such energy …' Then a shadow crossed her face and Ben knew she'd remembered. With a cross between a sigh and a groan, she hoisted herself out of the chair. 'Time to peel the spuds.'

As they peeled the potatoes together, Ben recalled Zaida's memories and the pictures on the Goldens' wall. Maybe everyone's grandparents deliberately stored layers of memories of their own distant, hard lives to re-tell as stories to their grandchildren?

* * *

The following Saturday, Ben slipped into Number 17, a little later than usual. The family had gone to the syna-gogue, but his money was on the mantelpiece and a slice of cake set out, as usual. Mossy, who'd been asleep on the armchair, jumped up, wagging his tail.

Starting work, Ben found the familiar routine helped him stop thinking about his mam. Maybe next week he'd see Hetty or Eddie, or hear more from Zaida. And what had happened to the refugee?

Then Mabel burst in. 'Ben, you're back!' she exclaimed. Pausing, she added awkwardly, 'Er … sorry about …' He nodded briefly, making it clear he didn't want to talk about it.

'I had to come home early,' she went on quickly, 'I've a streaming cold. The others have gone to Zaida and Bobba for Kiddush.' When he looked blank she explained, 'You know, the Sabbath blessing, wine and bread and kichels.'

Though she wasn't supposed to, she helped him clean the hearth. He offered her half the cake, which she didn't refuse. As they munched, she asked, 'Did you hear the war news?' He shook his head. For him the war, like everything else, had receded into the background. 'It said on the wireless that the Nazis invaded Russia!'

After a moment, he ventured, 'Is that bad?'

'Oh, you'd better ask Hetty,' she said. 'She knows all about the war.' Mopping her runny nose with a handkerchief, she went on uncertainly, 'Uncle Sam said it'll keep the Nazis busy fighting, because the Russians don't give up easily.'

'So the Nazis mightn't invade us or England?'

'Who knows?' she said. 'Uncle Sam hopes the Americans might come into the war to save us all. But poor Zaida's in a state. Hetty says that Lithuania, where he comes from, is in Russia, and he's worried about his family if the Nazis get there.'

'You mean the people in the photographs?' asked Ben. She looked at him in surprise. 'He told me about them,' he mumbled, embarrassed. 'Anyway, I'd better go.'

As he opened the door she said, sneezing, 'Everyone'll be glad you're back.'

He reached his own door, lifted his hand to open the latch, when it was opened for him by – his dad.

18

Heart to Heart

Hetty was getting dressed, pulling on her black lisle stockings and garters. Then, glancing at the weather house she noticed that the painted girl, instead of lurking inside as usual, had come right out. Hetty threw open the window, and, sure enough, after a spell of spring gales and showers the weather had turned suddenly warm, the sky chalk blue without a single cloud. She could leave off her chillproof vest and put on her ankle socks instead of the hated stockings. *And*, there was a day's holiday from school.

Mabel had finally left school and was training as a tailoress at Polikoff's along with Carmel, who'd just turned fourteen and also left school. It was hard, working from half-eight till six, but they were getting used to it, and, Hetty heard enviously, they were paid five shillings a week. According to Mabel, everyone sang as they worked, and apparently there was lots of giggling and chat about boyfriends.

On that matter, Michael had disappeared, but Hetty was now hearing a lot about Cyril, the tennis player with whom Mabel had played an unsuccessful doubles match at Carlisle, and who, Hetty suspected, wasn't much of an improvement on Michael.

So today Hetty revelled in having a day's freedom. She wanted to return to Dalkey and have another go at tracking down Renata. 'No one else is bothering,' she complained to Eddie. But even he seemed to have gone off the hunt, muttering, 'Da says they're working on it.'

Instead she'd agreed to go for a walk with Gertie to Herbert Park to see the baby ducklings and cygnets; or maybe to the zoo in Phoenix Park to see the newborn lion cub, if Gertie could scrounge the money.

But then Ma called from downstairs: 'Hetty! Good thing you're home today, I've a mountain of sewing. When you've finished the chores you can take Solly out for a walk in the sunshine.'

Hetty felt like Cinderella. Why did she never have time to herself? And now, with Mabel at work, it was worse.

* * *

Later, though, out in the fresh air with the gentle caress of the sun on her face, her resentment faded. Sitting erect, Solly eagerly watched the bustling street life around them, as Hetty, with Mossy at her heels, pushed the heavy pram up Stamer Street and into Harrington Street. A noisy tram clanged past; delivery boys' bikes, their baskets piled high with boxes and packages, wove in and out between lumbering carts. Solly shouted in excitement, pointing with his little fat finger as dogs ran barking in and out of the traffic.

A funeral carriage slowly passing by reminded her that she hadn't spoken to Ben since his mother had died. Her ma had called in to sympathise and had been welcomed by Granny with tea and a chat.

Though Hetty half-wanted to speak to Ben, she also dreaded it. What could you say? For a moment she tried to imagine life without Ma, and couldn't. Absorbed in her thoughts, she crossed the main road, avoiding a heavy brewer's dray pulled by two trudging workhorses.

Then, spilling out of the Triangle – the sweet shop at Kelly's Corner – a scuffling, larking crowd of Synge Street boys in black blazers and purple caps with gold crests appeared, engulfing Hetty, Mossy and the pram.

On the fringe of the crowd was Ben, his sandy hair flopping from under his cap, one cheek bulging with a gobstopper. He gazed at her in surprise, his brown eyes vulnerable, reminding her for a moment of the eyes of the puppies when she'd first seen them.

The puppies, the bombing, Ben's expression as he listened to Zaida's story, and the searing look she and Ben had exchanged – all this zoomed through her mind as Ben stood stock still, the crowd eddying around him and moving on, until he and Hetty were left standing opposite each other.

Forget the grievances, she told herself fiercely, and say something.

'I ... I'm sorry about your mother.' She looked intently at him, and again he saw real sympathy in the deep blue gaze he knew so well.

He struggled to reply, but no words came.

Solly started to grizzle and Hetty, confused by a strange mix of feelings, her heart inexplicably thumping, wheeled the pram around, mumbling, 'I'd better get back.'

But Ben had longed for an opportunity to talk to Hetty alone. It was now or never. Be brave, he urged himself. 'Er, I'd like ... um, could we ... maybe, go to that place, you know, where we saved Mossy and Flossy?'

So he did remember! She gave a brief nod, and Ben seized the handle of the pram. Together, to Solly's delight, they trundled it at top speed down Harrington Street and turned in the direction of the canal.

* * *

Ben stuffed his cap in his pocket, and spread out his well-worn school blazer, passed down from Sean and before that from Paddy, and they sat side by side on the grassy bank close to where the rescue had taken place. Solly, annoyed that his careering ride in the pram had come to an end, began to whimper and Hetty lifted him out to crawl around on the grass.

Ben reached out to pat the dog lying beside them, and

said, 'Remember that day?' It was hard to picture that frozen expanse. Now, ducks and moorhens were sailing among the reeds, tipping in and out of the water to excavate for tasty morsels.

'I thought you'd forgotten.' Hetty pulled the baby into her lap. 'I mean, you never even asked about the puppies!'

Forgotten? He said in a rush, 'No, it was just ...' But how could he repeat Dad's bitter words about the new neighbours? He muttered, 'It was hard times, my mam was sick, and my dad's a bit, you know ...' he stumbled on, 'well, he was worried, and angry, and now ... he's found out I'm working for you, and he doesn't ...' Unable to finish, his voice trailed off. He certainly couldn't tell her about the row that had followed when Dad had found him out and ranted on until Granny'd intervened and told Dad to leave Ben alone – 'the poor young fella, grieving for his mam.' Dad had stopped shouting and stumbled upstairs to the bedroom he used to share with Mam. After that there had been a sort of unspoken truce, with Dad not mentioning the job and even making an effort to be kinder to him.

Hetty said nothing at first, but somehow Ben felt she understood. They watched a swan gliding elegantly away under the canal bridge, leaving a rippling V in the bright water.

Hetty felt an unaccustomed sympathy. Ignoring his reference to his father, though she had a good idea what he really meant, she said quietly, 'If it hadn't been for you, the puppies would have died.'

'If it hadn't been for you, no one would have even tried to save them,' he replied, 'and you kept the two alive afterwards.' But the words 'died' and 'alive' tripped him up and brought him back to the present – the blackness, the emptiness, the fear …

Hetty said simply, 'You must miss your ma.'

He nodded silently and swallowed hard. But comforted by her presence and those few sympathetic words, he managed to pull himself together. At last they were relaxed in each other's presence. They both felt it.

Mossy raced down to the water, barking at the ducks scrambling hopefully up the bank, joyously chasing them back into the water amidst a chorus of resentful squawks. Solly laughed in delight.

Hetty started to get up. 'It's Solly's dinner time,' she explained. 'I need to get home.'

But Ben didn't budge. He knew he must find the courage to confess one more thing to her, otherwise how could they really be friends, with this remaining lie between them?

He forced the words out. 'Listen, er, I … I heard you and Eddie talking about the refugee.' She stared at him, the frown back in place. 'I couldn't help hearing,' he went on desperately, 'and ... and I even *nearly* reported her, but I–'

'You *what*?' Her shouted exclamation frightened Solly, who let out a yell. Hetty scrambled to her feet and lifted him into the pram, quickly strapping him in.

'Hetty! Wait!' Using her name felt strange. 'I *didn't* report her in the end. I even saw her calling to your house, I know now how risky it is for her ...'

Ignoring him she started wheeling Solly, red-faced and screaming, across the road.

As she gave the child his dummy, Ben, running to keep up, kept talking. 'Honestly, Hetty, please believe me. I nearly did something stupid, I didn't realise ... Uncle Matt explained it all, and Zaida, and now I understand.'

But she hurried on without speaking. I've lost her, he told himself flatly. I found her and I lost her.

And then, in despair, he thought of the words in Mam's last letter: she would always be there to help when she was needed. Mam, he said silently, as he followed Hetty homewards, help me now.

As they approached her house, Hetty turned to him, scowling, but at least talking to him.

'You ... you say you saw her. I s'pose you frightened her off?'

'No, no,' Ben almost shouted. 'I spotted her putting in

a note. I didn't want to scare her ...' He paused, then rushed on, 'Maybe I could help you find her somewhere safe and get her to her father.' After a moment he added, 'I helped before, remember?'

At first there was a chilling silence. But after a few moments she said distantly, but less angrily, 'I'll have to talk to Eddie.'

Ben drew a long breath. Surely Eddie would understand? 'Right,' he said softly, 'see you Saturday.'

As Hetty went into Number 17, Solly, all smiles now, waved 'Day-day', to him. Ben waved back.

Silently he said, Thanks, Mam, and went in home for his dinner.

19

For Whom the Bell Tolls

At home in Number 17 everyone was busy and Hetty didn't mention her meeting with Ben, though it stayed in her mind. It was always hard work preparing the family Passover meal, with matza crackers and wine and traditional foods, but Hetty usually enjoyed sitting around the table eating and drinking, and, interspersed with lots of family jokes, recounting the story of the miraculous escape of their ancestors, the Hebrew slaves, from Ancient Egypt to the Promised Land.

But this year it had all been a bit muted. Ma was preoccupied – orders for clothes and alterations were piling up, even with help from Carmel and Maureen's mother. 'Still,' Ma said, 'it brings in a few bob.' Da was still doing overtime work, and since his wage cut there'd been no more gambling, but everyone was tired and worried.

Hetty had to admit that even the few shillings Mabel earned helped with the rent. Lying on her bed after supper Mabel explained in detail that she was now learning CMT – cut, make and trim. 'But the days are awful long.' She yawned. 'And I really miss the crowd at school. Haven't seen Alison for ages.' Then, cheering up, she added, 'Still, lucky I've got Carmel and Maureen, and

Rebecca and the girls from Carlisle.'

'You were the one mad to leave and get work,' snapped Hetty, whose days seemed long as well, what with school, and extra chores due to Mabel's absence, messages for Ma, and minding Solly. And she was all too aware that *her* only real friends were her cousin Eddie and faithful Gertie. And maybe Ben?

'How's it going with Cyril?' she asked Mabel, forcing a pleasant tone.

Mabel, with less energy than usual, had started on her hair. 'Don't talk to me about Cyril,' she moaned. '*He's* only interested in his new Slazenger tennis racket. He didn't even ask me to the Passover Matza ramble.' Carefully pinning a curl, she added, 'I went with Rebecca and the other girls.'

'You don't *have* to go to things with a boy,' said Hetty scornfully. 'Anyway, it's only a picnic with matza crumbs everywhere. I went with Gertie, and it was fine. And Eddie, of course.'

'It doesn't count as going with a boy if he's your cousin,' said Mabel, equally scornfully.

'You better not tell Eddie he doesn't count!' snapped Hetty. She gazed out of the window at the yard, where Ma's marigolds struggled for life in the cracks in the concrete. 'Anyway, at least Passover's finished now – no more matza!'

'Ma gave some to the neighbours, even next door,' said Mabel, in good humour again, 'and I brought a packet in to the girls in work.' She finished her curls. '*They* all liked them.'

'They don't have to eat them for eight days like us.' Still, Hetty wondered if Ben had tried the crackers. She'd ask him next time they met.

* * *

At Number 19, Ben had also kept quiet about his talk with Hetty, which had warmed his heart. These days he was struggling with dreams of Mam. Sometimes when he woke his pillow was wet with tears. He tried to call up the memory of her smiling in her summery yellow dress, Dad's arm around her. But the image that lingered was of Mam on the veranda in Crooksling, her eyes too bright, her thin cheeks too flushed, feebly raising her hand to wave as they left, with the golden-haired girl sitting up in the next bed.

Puzzling over the strange quotation Mam had inscribed in his autograph book: 'Never send to know for whom the bell tolls, it tolls for thee', he asked Uncle Matt what it meant. 'Think about it, Ben,' Uncle Matt replied, pulling Ben close as he sat in the *súgán* chair nursing his bad leg, his war injury, which swelled up from time to time so that he had to use a stick. 'Here's a clue: the poet who wrote that, John Donne, was lying sick when he heard the church bell toll. That meant someone had died.'

Ben thought while Granny made tea. After a while he shouted triumphantly, 'I know! You have to care about what's happening to other people in case it happens to you.'

Uncle Matt clapped him on the back. 'Almost right! What's really important is to care about and help people in trouble as if their problems were your own.'

He nudged Granny and she ruffled Ben's hair and said approvingly, 'A chip off the old block!'

When Dad arrived home from work and they all sat down to Granny's shepherd's pie, Uncle Matt asked Dad, 'Comin' to the Trade Union protest tomorrow, Stephen?' He tapped his bad leg. 'I can't march, but if you're going early, Sean and Ben could come with me.'

'Ah sure, I might follow on with Sean.' Dad was evasive. 'We'll see you and Ben there later.' That meant he was going for a few drinks.

'We could have a jar afterwards,' said Uncle Matt quietly. But Dad was opening the *Evening Mail*.

In bed, Ben reflected about the tolling bell. Was Mam telling him that, whatever about his dad, he, Ben, must try to help the refugee girl? Some of his sadness had fallen away at the possibility of doing something brave and important with Hetty again, and seeing that vivid light in her blue eyes.

In the morning, as always, the yearning for Mam was still with him – 'seas of sorrow' as Granny once put it when she'd heard him sobbing and come into his room and hugged him.

Yet last night he'd had no dreams, and in the morning the pillow was dry.

20

The Protest

All over Dublin there were huge posters announcing the mass demonstration against the anti-trade union Bill.

'Did ya hear, Ben, there's fifty-three unions marching from Mountjoy Square, with bands an' all?' said Smiler excitedly when he called for Ben. 'They're all ending up in College Green for the big rally.'

The two set off together for Uncle Matt's. Smiler had his grey 'steelier' marble in his pocket, but Ben, though the conker season was long over, still had his 'sixer'; fingering its knobbly contours reminded him of happier times.

When they reached Ovoca Road, Auntie Bridie gave them thick slices of soda bread with jam 'in case they got a bit peckish'.

Uncle Matt muttered to Ben, 'Got a bit of not-so-good news. I haven't told Gran yet, she has grief enough as it is.' He paused. 'Fact is, our Paddy's ship was torpedoed by enemy U-boats. It was damaged, but they managed to get back to port.'

'Was Paddy hurt?' asked Ben anxiously.

'Bit of shrapnel. We think it's only a flesh wound, thanks be to God. I'm sure he'll be fine.' Biting on his clay pipe, he went on, 'He's in hospital in Liverpool. We're going over to bring him home for his sick leave, I'll tell Granny then.' He grinned reassuringly, but Ben could see the worry in his eyes.

Ben realised that since his mother's death he'd almost forgotten about the war that was raging and the soldiers, many Irish like Paddy, fighting the Nazis. Wishing he could find better words, he told Uncle Matt, 'Tell him I was asking for him.'

* * *

College Green was solid with people jostling on the footpaths, leaning out of office windows and climbing on to walls and railings to get a better view.

Such was the crush that Ben, Smiler and Uncle Matt were carried along by the crowd, mostly men and boys, towards the imposing stone entrance of Trinity College. 'We'll never meet your dad or Sean in this,' said Uncle Matt.

There was a roar from the crowd and Uncle Matt helped Ben shin up an already crowded lamp post, and then hoisted Smiler up.

A voice shouted, 'Look, it's Big Jim Larkin! He's going to speak!'

'That fella's afraid of nobody,' said another man. 'He'll tell them how the working man's being squeezed dry.'

Far away across the sea of caps and hats Ben spied a

wooden platform with a row of seated union and Labour leaders. A tall, vigorous man, speaking passionately into a microphone on a metal tripod, was waving a copy of the anit-trade union Bill in the air. They heard snatches: down with the wages standstill' … 'a fair day's work for a fair day's pay' … 'must rely on ourselves' ... punctuated by yells of approval from the crowd.

And then, like a conjuror, the speaker swept a match from his pocket, set the Bill alight and held it aloft in flames. The crowd cheered wildly.

A few more speeches, then it was over. Ben slid down the lamp post. His mam, he knew, wouldn't have missed this for the world.

A sudden shower speeded the dispersing crowds. As they shoved their way towards George's Street, Smiler, spying his older cousin ahead in the crowd, said, 'See ya', and ran to catch him up.

'No sign of your dad or Sean,' said Uncle Matt. 'Though it's hard to see anyone in this crowd.' The rain grew heavier. Their jackets soaked, they took shelter with a group of others under a tree.

An unmistakable voice behind them said, 'Isn't that our *Shabbos goy*?' Ben whirled round. Zaida, in the old great-coat which he seemed to wear always, summer and winter, black skullcap on his silver hair, was holding up a large umbrella. Huddling under it were Eddie, Hetty's da

– and Hetty herself, wrapped in an old rubber mackintosh, not exactly grinning, but not frowning either.

Trust Hetty, thought Ben with delight, to be one of the few females at the protest.

'Come on,' cried Zaida, 'there's room for us all under this umbrella!' There wasn't really, but they squeezed in anyway.

Ben, relieved that his dad and Sean weren't around, felt a wave of gladness at the sight of the Goldens. He still wasn't sure if, after his confession to Hetty, she and Eddie would accept him as a friend. Wanting to be their friend as well as their *Shabbos goy* was something that had seemed unthinkable a few months earlier. But now he wanted it more than anything.

* * *

Uncle Matt, looking pleased, asked the Goldens, 'So you're all union supporters?'

'Of course, from years back when we were new immigrants,' said Zaida proudly. 'Tailors' assistants only earned a few shillings a week, and I could hardly speak English, but so many of us joined the Garment Workers' Union that they called it the Jewish Union.'

'My wages were cut recently,' murmured Hetty's da, 'and decent wages is what the unions are fighting for, so here we are.'

Uncle Matt nodded sympathetically.

The rain had lessened and they started walking up George's Street towards home. Uncle Matt mentioned the Nazi invasion of Russia. 'At least it'll weaken the Nazis,' said Hetty's da. 'The Russians are strong fighters.'

'The Nazis have bitten off more than they can chew,' agreed Uncle Matt. 'It could do for them in time, though I know it's not going so well for us now.'

Zaida said anxiously, 'I worry in case the Nazis get to my little *shtetl*, Akmiyan.' His voice shook. 'I haven't heard from the family for so long.'

Uncle Matt put a strong hand on the old man's shoulder. 'Surely they'll be all right?' he said. 'The Nazis wouldn't bother with a small village.'

Zaida sighed. 'I'm not so sure. The Nazis ... there's no end to their evil, their killing ... They want to conquer the world.'

* * *

Following behind, Ben and Hetty slowed their pace so Eddie could keep up. He murmured to Ben, 'Hetty told me you saw the refugee girl.'

'That's right,' said Ben quickly. 'But don't worry, I said nothing–'

But before he could finish, a tall, slim girl, her fair hair bundled under a beret, hurried up to them. Staring at

Zaida's skull cap, she addressed him in a low foreign-accented voice. 'Er, excuse please, you are of ze Jewish people?'

Taken aback, Zaida reached out his hand. 'Yes, my dear,' he said gently. 'Can I help you?'

They all watched, dumbfounded.

The image of the refugee girl Ben had nearly reported and later spotted in Martin Street, had been driven from his mind, along with much else, by his mother's death. But now the girl was here beside them, thin, strained and obviously frightened – his interest and involvement came flooding back. Her eyes, shadowed with fear, were like those of a hunted animal.

Glancing at Ben and Uncle Matt, Zaida told her, 'Perhaps we can talk at my house.'

She looked anxiously around the group. 'But I must soon catch bus!'

'You can trust us,' Uncle Matt said quietly to Zaida.

'I know,' said Zaida. 'Perhaps together we can help this young lady.'

Hetty broke in excitedly, 'She's Renata Stern, a refugee from the Nazis.' Turning to the girl, she asked, 'Did you get the message we left at the house?'

'House?' Hetty's da looked puzzled. 'What house? How did you know where she was?'

But Hetty was saying urgently to Renata, 'Come home

with us, we can hide you.'

'Yes, I would like, but I must first go to lodgings, to get sewing machine ...' She glanced nervously over her shoulder. They had to listen hard to understand as she explained she was from Berlin, her father was in a town in Ireland but they'd lost touch. Meanwhile her visa had long ago run out and she could be deported. 'Somebody tell me Jewish people here maybe help. But I oblige move my lodgings. When I go back for sewing machine, I find Hetty note.' She glanced at her gratefully. 'I do not know where is zis Portobello, I afraid ask in case ...'

As they stood listening in an entranced circle, a young Guard approached. 'Move along, now. Protest's over,' he said pleasantly. 'Have ye no homes to go to?'

Renata's eyes widened, and before anyone could stop her she fled down a laneway. 'Oh no!' wailed Hetty. 'We haven't got her address, and now she's gone.' She dashed after her.

Ben wanted to follow, but Uncle Matt stopped him. 'No point everyone rushing after her, it'll just draw more attention.'

Suddenly, realising the secret was out, everyone started to speak at once, Eddie explaining to Hetty's da and Zaida, and Ben to Uncle Matt, about the search for Renata.

'To be a refugee and alone,' said Zaida, sadly. 'It is hard ... and for such a young girl ...'

Gazing after Renata and Hetty, Uncle Matt said, admiringly, 'Still, two determined young ones there.'

Minutes later, Hetty returned alone. 'I couldn't find her,' she muttered to the circle of expectant faces, and burst into tears.

Eddie put his arm round her. 'Don't worry, Hetty,' he said gently. 'We may not have *her* address, but don't forget, she has yours!'

21

The Visitor

The Saturday after the protest was cold with heavy rain clouds. There had been no further news about Renata, and Hetty was distraught.

Ben, alone in the Goldens' house, was lighting the last fire of the season, and wondering about Paddy in Liverpool, and how badly wounded he was. Then his thoughts moved to his mam, back down into the well of grief that was always with him. Would he ever stop missing her and get used to the gaping hole that had opened up in his life?

These days Dad was mostly silent – 'his way of grieving,' Granny had said – but with occasional unexpected gestures of comfort to Ben – a pat on the shoulder, a ruffle of his hair. He'd never mentioned Ben's job again, and Ben wondered if he'd changed towards the Jewish neighbours. At least he'd been polite to those who'd called to sympathise.

Ben himself knew now that, apart from small things like customs or festivals or foods, the so-called 'foreign' neighbours weren't really that different from themselves. They might pray in a different way, but they had the same joys and sorrows and troubles. Surely Dad and Sean would come to see that too?

What made Ben feel bitter was that neither Dad nor Sean mentioned Mam, almost as though she'd never existed. Granny was the only one Ben could talk to about her, recalling the good times. When he confided that he had trouble picturing her as she was before her illness, Granny had placed an old photo on the mantelpiece; it was cracked and a little faded, but Mam was smiling in her yellow dress, a tiny hat with a wisp of veiling and high-heeled white shoes.

Ben felt comforted. And though Dad never mentioned it, Ben noticed that one day he'd put it in a frame.

* * *

Kneeling to poke the fire in Number 17, Ben heard a gentle tap on the door – surely too early for the family's return? A neighbour? Or perhaps …? He hurried to open the door.

Renata stood there, her hair plastered down by the rain. Ben threw an anxious glance down the wet street as he ushered her in, taking her battered suitcase and heavy sewing machine, and seating her in Leon Golden's sagging armchair. She looked exhausted, and Ben, knowing what Granny would do, hastened to make her a cup of tea with the used tea-leaves from the tin. Peering into the breadbin he cut off a hunk of the fresh Sabbath bread, hoping it wasn't going to get him into trouble with anyone. He paused, then added the slice of cake left out for him.

Gratefully, Renata gulped the tea and wolfed down the food. 'That is good,' she said with a little smile. 'Er, Hetty, she not here?'

'She'll be back soon.'

She seemed to understand, and as the room grew warm she unbuttoned her worn cardigan, closed her eyes, and instantly fell asleep.

Instead of leaving Number 17 when he had finished work, Ben remained, watching over the sleeping girl, observing the worry lines on her forehead. If he'd reported her that day, Uncle Matt had explained, she'd have been sent to Belfast and possibly to England, and there, if you were German and over seventeen you'd be classified as an enemy alien and maybe imprisoned or deported.

Thankfully his uncle had put him right. Now, of course, he and Auntie Bridie had the heartache of Paddy being wounded. As soon as they returned from Liverpool, Ben decided he'd go straight round to see them.

The sudden rattle of the lock signalled the family's return. Ben rushed to the door, finger on his lips. They all crept in.

When Hetty saw Renata asleep in the chair, the empty mug and plate beside her, she turned to Ben. As before, the look held between them. She stepped towards him, and for a wild moment he thought she was going to hug him. But she stopped short and mumbled, 'Thanks ... I mean, for looking after her and ... well, you know ...'

The moment passed. Still, Ben was invited to the Sabbath lunch, the 'cholent' that had been cooking slowly on the range since the night before. Knowing Granny was at a church cake sale, and Dad and Sean were at work, Ben, pleased but slightly nervous, accepted.

Renata, only now realising Ben wasn't a family member, eyed him suspiciously, but Eddie told her: 'It's all right. He's a friend.' She glanced for confirmation at Hetty, who nodded. Though she was unsmiling, Ben knew she'd forgiven him.

At the meal, Renata said little but ate ravenously. Then she slept again, in Hetty's bed upstairs. After lunch, Eddie went home. 'I'll tell Da about Renata, he'll talk to the Refugee Committee,' he told Hetty. 'I'll be back later.'

Then, as Ben left, Hetty followed him to the door. 'You come back too, Ben, you're in this now.' She added in her bossy way, 'Mind – not a word to anyone!'

Strolling the few steps to his house, he realised it was the first time she'd used his name. Energised and excited at being involved with something so important, he recalled Eddie once saying to him, 'Hetty makes you do things you'd never do yourself.'

As Ben entered Number 19, Sean was just coming out. 'Still doing that boring Sabbath job, Specky?'

'*Ben*, to you,' he replied coolly, and stalked into the house, leaving Sean gazing after him, puzzled and a little put out.

* * *

Later on, Hetty's parents sat expectantly with Bobba and Zaida in the parlour of Number 17, with Eddie, Hetty and Ben on the floor and Solly crawling about, as Renata told her story.

She described her family in Berlin and explained that her father was a doctor. 'He have patients from all religions,' she told them. 'And us children, we have Christian friends, Jewish friends, it not matter. We are happy.' Her voice trembled. 'In Berlin in summer people sit in open-air cafés with talk and music, children playing. It was–' she stopped, remembering. 'But then Hitler and Nazis were – how do you say – elect? And everything change.' Her grey-green eyes were full of tears.

'Don't distress yourself, my dear,' said Zaida gently, handing her a handkerchief.

But Renata, mopping her eyes, said, 'No, it is good for me to have somebody to tell ...'

She told them about the prison camps, and how Jews were gradually dehumanised and everything they owned stolen by the Nazis.

'They take our furniture, bicycle, wireless, camera,' she said. 'Later even Papa's stethoscope, and Minka, our little cat. In the end we have ... nothing.'

She continued, in a whisper, 'On our coats all Jews, small children too, must wear yellow star with "*Jude*" on it.' The words seemed torn from her. 'My brother Walter get away on boat to Palestine. In Berlin Nazis do not let Jews work as doctor. After long time Papa get visa to work in factory in Ireland, at, er, Lang Vord?'

They shook their heads, puzzled. 'Longford?' tried Da.

'Ya, Longford. They make there–' searching for the word, she pointed to her head.

'Hats?' 'Caps?' 'Wigs?' 'Ribbons?', they chorused, laughing to lighten the tragic story. Renata, with a quick smile, nodded at 'ribbons', her hair, now dry, falling down her shoulders like a golden silk net.

In Longford her father was refused entry visas for Ireland for the rest of the family. Meanwhile from Berlin the family fled to Warsaw ...

Renata's voice was growing hoarse, as they sat, frozen, listening.

'It's enough!' Da jumped up, agitated. 'This is too upsetting.'

'For her, Da, or for us?' asked Hetty sharply. He glared at her, but Renata insisted, 'You *must* hear, too many not want to know. And it not so far away ...' She shivered, and they all, Hetty cuddling Mossy to her, felt the sudden chill.

'You must rest your voice, dear,' Ma said soothingly to Renata. 'We'll have a hot drink.'

In the kitchen, even Mabel was subdued, murmuring hesitantly, 'At least we're safe here–'

'If the Nazis don't invade,' declared Hetty. How could anyone, listening to Renata's story, feel safe? For some reason she felt glad that Ben, quietly listening, was there with them.

As they brought in the hot shell cocoa, Bobba said to her son, 'Surely, Leon, we can listen to a girl whose life has been torn apart?'

'We must all know,' Zaida agreed, 'what the Nazis do in Germany, in Poland – and everywhere they rule.' Ben and Hetty both followed his glance up at the photographs from Lithuania with the serious children and the grandmother holding the baby.

Ma carried Solly in from the kitchen, clutching his bottle, to say good night. As Renata hugged him, her face was transformed and they saw her, not as a refugee, harried and troubled, but as a beautiful, serene young girl.

22

Shelter

'In Warsaw,' Renata told them later, 'no one ever smile. Always we are in fear. Then my father arrange letter to me from aunt in Ireland saying she must see me before she died–'

'You have an aunt here?' asked Ma, surprised.

Renata shook her head. 'No, it was a …'

'A fabrication?' put in Da.

A white lie, thought Ben, to save a life.

'But it worked?' asked Mabel.

Renata nodded. 'Every day people stand in long lines for visas, like Berlin. But Mutti show the letter, and also bribe official with gold wedding ring she had hide, and I get visa for Ireland, four week only.' She pulled a tattered piece of paper from her pocket, the typed words and official stamps and signatures faded and smudged. 'Now I am … this word I know … illegal.'

'But how did you get to Dalkey?' asked Eddie.

Caught up in her story, speaking faster and faster, she described the difficult journey by train and boat, finally reaching what she called 'Dun Lerry', meaning Dun Laoghaire. She stayed first in a room near the ferry terminal. 'I have little money left. I write my father, but his address in Long Ford, it is change. Then,' she went on, 'two men from the Department of Extra– how you say?'

'External Affairs?' asked Ma.

'Yes, they call, they say I must leave. And the next day, I see big letters in paper: NAZIS BOMB WARSAW! They march into Poland.' She clutched Zaida's handkerchief tightly. 'Later I sit on bus with my things, thinking what will happen to my family now Nazis are in Warsaw? I am weeping, and a kind lady show me in a newspaper, Rooms To Let.'

She rented a room in Dalkey, where the family was good to her. 'They help me get sewing machine on HP, paying each week, and I do alterations and get some money. They teach me English too. But one day I see man was police.'

'Did he give you away?' asked Hetty.

Renata shook her head. 'No, he ask me stay, with smaller rent because of my trouble. But there is too much risk for me, also for his job.'

So I misjudged that man, thought Hetty, as she and Eddie exchanged glances.

'I move to small, cheap room in basement. It is dark, blankets are damp. I fear to tell my address.'

She paused for breath, and Mabel burst out, 'We're always complaining about stupid things that don't matter, and look at all you've been through!'

Hetty's eyes met Ben's. He'd lost his mam. That was something that did matter. Hetty had the sensation again of a special link between them, that each knew what the other was thinking.

'Did you get letters from your family?' Eddie asked Renata.

'After war start in Poland there are not any more letters …' her voice faded so they could hardly hear her. 'I do not know what happen to Mutti and Ella and Papa's family in Warsaw, or Walter. I do not even know where is my father, perhaps he has left ribbon factory. I must find him, he is all left of my family …' She gave a deep shuddering sigh, her head drooping like a flower after heavy rain.

For moments they were all silent. What could you say? Into Ben's mind crept Granny's words: 'seas of sorrow'.

* * *

As Da rose to leave for the evening service, he touched Renata's shoulder kindly. 'I'll see Sam in the synagogue,' he muttered, 'maybe Renata can stay with them.'

'I'm sure that'd be all right–' said Eddie eagerly.

But Hetty chimed in, 'Why can't she stay with us?'

'Quiet, Hetty,' snapped Da. 'We have to think this through. There are dangers – and things are not so easy for us now.'

As the door slammed behind him, Ma said slowly to

Eddie, 'You know, I'm not sure Renata *should* go to your house. Sam's on the Refugee Committee, and he's a leader of the community. It's a higher risk.'

'Sarah is right.' Zaida got up and put his arm round Renata. 'To the immigration people our Renata is an "illegal alien". Better not in Sam's house.'

Hetty nodded vigorously as Zaida went on, 'Bobba and I have not much room, but we will pay happily from our savings for Renata's keep.' Everyone waited for Bobba's usual sharp response, but she said quietly, 'Of course, we must all help.'

'The Refugee Committee might help too,' put in Eddie. 'I'll ask Da.'

'Then it's settled,' Hetty declared quickly. 'Renata must stay here. She can have my bed.' She glanced at Ma. 'Da'll come around, won't he?' Ma said nothing, but gave a tiny smile, and Hetty knew she would persuade him.

'Still, we have to remember the dangers,' warned Eddie. 'Someone might spot her, word could get out.'

'We'll be very careful.' Hetty took Renata's hand. 'If you can stay hidden here till the fuss dies down, then we can help you find your father.'

There was agreement all round.

Mossy, curled on the hearthrug, woke up, shook himself, then went over to Renata, who had been listening as the discussion seethed around her, and pushed his wet nose into her hand.

Stroking his velvety head, she murmured, 'I thank you *mit meinem ganzen Herz.*' She held out her hands to them all with a wide smile. 'In English, I think – with all of my heart.'

'It's like a film,' said Mabel dreamily, adding hastily, 'except, of course, it's real.' Hetty and Ben exchanged a grin.

Hiding her emotion, Renata said, 'Also I have machine. I could help with sewing?'

Ma smiled, and, pointing to the heap of clothing on the shelf, said a heartfelt, 'Oh, yes!'

* * *

But when Da returned from the synagogue with Uncle Sam, their faces were grave. Uncle Sam went straight to Renata. 'I'm happy to meet you, my dear.' He shook her hand. 'Leon's told me some of your story. You've shown such courage.' He cleared his throat. 'But I must tell you, I heard today from the Committee that immigration officers are now on the trail of what they call "an illegal female refugee known to be in the Portobello area".'

Renata, pale as a marble statue, whispered, 'All I hope is short time till I find Papa.' She clasped her hands tightly together. 'But I am fear they look for me now in Jewish homes in Portobello.'

Uncle Sam sat down heavily. 'I'm afraid time is not on our side–'

He was interrupted by a knock on the front door. A tremor ran through the room. Renata leapt up from her seat. Putting a finger to her lips, Ma went quietly to the door and called, 'Who is it?'

Inside the crowded parlour, as Mabel clutched her hand, Hetty thought, this must be what it's like for Jews waiting for the Nazi SS to burst in. But, of course, this wasn't Germany and the Nazis weren't here. Ma opened the door, and they heard friendly voices, even a laugh.

Coming back in, she said, 'It's all right, just Carmel to borrow a cup of sugar.' But her face was pale. 'I told her you'd pop over later, Mabel.'

Hetty could see Renata was trembling. 'It's all right, Renata, it's only a friend,' she said soothingly. 'Even if they knew you were here, they wouldn't tell anyone,' she added.

Hetty hoped that was true. But all of them, especially Ben, were aware that though most of the neighbours would keep silent, there might always be *somebody* who would tell.

* * *

Zaida and Bobba hugged everyone and then the frail old couple went off arm-in-arm. Before he left, Uncle Sam told them the Refugee Committee was trying to arrange for Renata to go north to Millisle, the refugee farm in County Down which sheltered young people who'd escaped from Europe on Kindertransports.

'But that's taking her even further away from her father,' Hetty protested to Eddie, who'd stayed behind.

Through Renata's sad recital and then the sudden knock at the door, Ben had said little. But, as he became increasingly aware of her danger in Number 17, an idea gradually took shape in his mind. He knew it was risky, maybe it just wasn't possible. But he owed it to Renata to try.

He said quietly to Eddie, beside him, 'D'you think she'd be safer in a house that wasn't Jewish?'

Eddie hesitated. 'Well, I s'pose so.'

Ben continued slowly, 'Maybe she could stay with my Uncle Matt and Auntie Bridie? They're in Ovoca Road, on the edge of Portobello. There aren't many ...' he stopped, embarrassed.

Hetty finished, 'Not so many Jewish families there.' Her blue eyes had lit up, sparkling. 'That could be a help.'

Ben stumbled on, 'The thing is, they're only coming back from Liverpool on the mail boat today with my cousin, Paddy. He's been wounded, and I'd have to ask them.'

'Your cousin's fighting in the war?' Da, who usually avoided Ben, was impressed.

But already Ben could see problems he hadn't thought of. How badly injured *was* Paddy? Maybe the family had enough to worry about? And what if his dad found out and did what he himself had once tried to do? Or Sean?

Renata, Hetty and Eddie looked at him gratefully, but Ben was asking himself, how did I get into this?

As he left Number 17, a figure loomed beside him in the rain-swept street. He jumped, but it was only Mabel's current boyfriend – who was short and plump and had replaced tennis-mad Cyril – arriving with a bunch of flowers. Ben called Mabel urgently and she came rushing out, looking anxious.

Hetty appeared in the hall, rolled her eyes, then grinned at Ben, and firmly closed the door behind them all, while Mabel gabbled to the puzzled visitor, pushing him back into the street, 'Oh, what a surprise, er, lovely flowers, I'm afraid we can't go inside because … er, someone's sort of sick …'

Another white lie, thought Ben. This was all going to be very tricky.

He decided, as usual, to go to Granny first. With her help, maybe he could finally play his longed-for part in the rescue of Renata, and make Hetty happy – and his mam proud.

23

If Not Now, When?

As he pushed open the front door, Ben's confidence was already draining away. To his immense relief only Granny was home, dozing in the *súgán* chair, the socks she had been darning in a heap in her lap, the wireless chattering unheard beside her, a sponge cake she had bought at a church sale on the table.

Ben made a cup of tea. As he put it down beside her she woke, smiled with an effort, and said softly, 'Well, Benny pet, what trouble are ye in now?'

As she sipped the weak tea he related Renata's story. Listening, her expression was full of sympathy. 'God help that poor young girl – and Matt and Bridie not back yet with Paddy, though I'm sure they'll help.' She sighed. 'If only Marie was here ...'

'But she will be here when we need her,' said Ben. 'She said so in that letter.'

Granny smiled sadly. 'So she did, pet.' Then she looked beyond Ben and her face changed. He whirled around.

Under cover of the wireless, while they were absorbed in Ben's story, his father had silently entered the room and was leaning against the wall, an ugly expression on his face.

There was a tense silence. Granny closed her eyes, as if summoning strength. As always, when faced with Dad's anger, a sick fear began to course through Ben.

'So, I come home early from the pub, like you're always telling me, and ye're busy hatching plots behind my back!' Dad grinned bitterly. 'And ye're going to save this young one, this "refugee" – more likely a spy – and keep her here where she doesn't belong, and put us all in danger wit' your sentimental rubbish.'

Granny stood, small and indomitable. 'Listen here to me, Stephen, it's not sentimental to try and save a young girl, wherever she's from, and whatever her religion.'

'And she's *not* a spy–' Ben tried to say.

But Dad's rage was building up as it always did. 'I'm going for the Guards!' he shouted.

At that point, Sean came in, dragging his bike, so taken aback by what was going on that he said nothing, just stared.

They all stood there, like a scene in a play. Into Ben's terrified heart a word flashed like a beam from a searchlight. Courage. He must summon it up. He had learned that you could show courage in small ways – like Mam's loving cheerfulness when she was so ill; Granny, losing her daughter but finding the strength to take care of the family; the golden-haired girl in the sanatorium; Hetty, determined to help Renata even if it got her into trouble;

Eddie, ready to help her, and also friendly and funny despite his damaged leg; and, of course, Renata, battling alone in a strange land to find her father. It was his turn to find the courage to face his father, and he knew now it was in him.

As all this flickered through his mind he stood up straight. He must show his dad that he wasn't just a frightened little boy, that he too had courage.

At first his throat seemed to have closed. But though his heart was thumping, he said quietly to Dad, 'All we're asking–'

But Dad snarled: 'So it's *we* now is it? Let me remind you that us here, *we're* your family, not that crowd next door.'

'Of course they're not my family.' Ben kept his voice even. 'They just want to help this girl stay till she finds her father.' He noted that despite his bluster, Dad hadn't actually banged out and gone for the Guards.

Struggling on, ignoring Dad's interruptions, willing him to listen, he outlined Renata's story. And from somewhere the words came to him and his panic was held at bay until he had finished. 'It's dangerous for her next door with people knocking at the door an' all, so we're asking Uncle Matt and Auntie Bridie to take her in, but they're not back yet.'

For a moment no one spoke. Ben was aware of Sean

looking at him with the same sort of grudging respect as when Ben had first told him about the job in the Goldens.

Dad growled, 'And who decided to bring Matt into all this?'

To Ben's relief, Granny seized the moment. 'Never mind that now. We all know Matt and Bridie wouldn't refuse to give an unfortunate girl shelter, whoever she is.' Her voice trembled. 'And neither would poor Marie, God love her, if she was here.'

Granny had made a telling point. Dad crumpled like a burst balloon into the *súgán* chair, his expression changing from rage, to wariness, to sadness. 'Yes … poor Marie …' And echoing Granny, 'If only she was here.'

Sean broke in impatiently. 'If you're waiting on Uncle Matt to take in the girl,' he demanded of Ben, 'where's she going till he gets back?'

'Well, she's not coming here,' grunted Dad, but his rage had sputtered out.

'Well, I hope Uncle Matt comes soon, so,' Sean said, wheeling his bike through the house and out the back. 'I'm starving with the hunger.'

Granny hurried into the kitchen, murmuring to Ben, 'Don't worry, pet, it'll be all right. You go and get that girl as soon as we've finished. I'll make up a mattress on the floor in my room.'

'She's called Renata,' whispered Ben joyfully.

* * *

Granny made a pot of tea, and, as if the row had never happened, Sean related in detail how he'd learned to staunch a bleeding wound, put a broken leg in a splint, and revive someone who'd passed out; he didn't seem to mind that there was no great interest.

They all brightened up when Granny brought in the jam sponge. Offering the first slice to Dad, she announced quietly but firmly, 'Until Matt gets back, that young one's to come here.' Dad half-rose, then sank back and shrugged, muttering, 'We could end up in jail for this, lose the job ...' But it was only a token protest. Ben felt calmer, as though a violent storm had threatened, buffeted them briefly, and then passed.

When Sean got his bike out to go off to a late-night ARP shift, Granny reminded him, 'Remember what Uncle Matt said to you that time. Not a word, mind.'

'Ah, sure, I've more important things to be doing,' he replied. 'Anyways, I can keep a secret if I hafta.' As he passed Ben he hissed, 'Specky, I never knew you had it in you,' and slammed the door before Ben could say a word.

Dad sat on in the *súgán* chair, finishing the paper, as Ben helped Granny wash up.

'It's late. Matt and Bridie should be here by now,' worried Granny. 'I hope Paddy's all right.' She had addressed Dad, and he muttered, 'Sure, the mail boat's always late these days.'

Ben whispered to Granny, 'I'm going in to get Renata.'

'Right, pet.' Raising her voice she added, 'And I want her to have the kind of welcome we're known for in Ireland.'

Dad looked up. 'What's done is done, I suppose,' he said grudgingly. 'I'm off to bed. I'll keep my mouth shut, for the sake of Marie, but that girl needn't expect a *céad míle fáilte* from me.'

Ben smiled to himself. They'd never be able to explain 'a hundred thousand welcomes' to Renata anyway.

* * *

But when he stepped outside, a nasty shock awaited him. In the rainy night, he watched in dismay as three figures left the Goldens' house, walking towards the South Circular Road – a uniformed Guard and another man, with the slender figure of Renata between them, clutching her suitcase.

He was too late! Ben, devastated, and guessing the state Hetty would be in, was desperate to rush in to Number 17 and find out what had happened.

But Granny, who came up behind him, touched his arm. From the opposite direction Uncle Matt was hurrying towards them, with Auntie Bridie tottering in her high heels, and Paddy between them, on crutches.

Ben turned back to watch Renata until all he could see in the gloom was the distant bright sheen of her hair. Then, knowing he couldn't leave now to find out what had happened, he forced himself to join in the welcome for Paddy.

24

Caught

In Number 19 that evening, just before the gas had gone off, Granny had cooked Matt and his family a big fry for their homecoming and did her best to keep it warm on the glimmer. As they tucked in, Paddy showed them his bandaged leg and explained how a piece of shrapnel had sliced into him when his ship was attacked by U-boats.

'You could see torpedoes slithering through the water towards you,' he said, bruises discolouring his face. 'There were explosions all around the convoy.'

'Poor lad, God love you,' said Granny. 'Such a world – war, refugees, violence everywhere!'

'Is it … does the leg hurt a lot?' Ben asked hesitantly. But even Paddy's narrow escape from serious wounds, or worse, couldn't quite blot out the image of Renata and the two officers walking away down the road.

'It's not bad. I was lucky. We shook 'em off, but one of my mates w-was …' Paddy stopped, swallowing hard. 'He was from Belfast.' Auntie Bridie put her arms around him, and Uncle Matt covered Paddy's hand with his. 'Your mate fell in the line of duty,' he said gently. 'It's against terrible evil that you're fighting.'

'Still, many poor souls are grieving tonight,' said Granny quietly.

As the hungry visitors ate, the mood lightened. Dad came downstairs, greeted Matt and Bridie, gripped Paddy's shoulder warmly and enquired about his injury. He seemed in much better form, as if the row with Ben and Granny had somehow cleared the air. 'Glad to be home, eh?' he asked Paddy.

Paddy grinned. 'It'd be even better without those oul' birds.' Auntie Bridie nodded in silent agreement, and Matt chewed his pipe impassively as Ben and Granny smiled.

What Ben wanted now was to talk to his uncle about Renata. After the row they'd just had, he expected Dad, at best, to ignore him, but to his astonishment Dad said casually, 'Matt, Ben here wants to ask you about this girl who needs a home.' He didn't use the word 'refugee', but added, with the ghost of a smile, 'There's been a lot going on here tonight.'

Ben briefly told Renata's story. When they heard he'd seen her being taken away only an hour earlier, they were all shocked. Even Dad was silenced.

'We'd have taken her in.' Uncle Matt was upset. 'She'd have been safer in Ovoca Road.'

'We'd never turn away a young girl in trouble,' agreed Auntie Bridie.

'It would've been nice,' said Paddy quietly. 'A sort of foster sister.'

'You never know,' put in Granny. 'Maybe she'll get away. She knows where to come now.'

But Ben still felt an overwhelming sadness at what had happened after all their efforts – and guilt. If only he'd called for her earlier …

As the family left to go home, Uncle Matt took him aside. 'Benny,' he said gently, 'you've grown up these last weeks, the hard way. However it turns out, you tried to do the right thing this time, and I'm proud of you – and so would your mam be.'

* * *

As soon as he could the next morning, Ben called to the Golden house. Hetty opened the door. There was no one else up.

'I'm really sorry, I was just coming for her–' Ben began.

But she said quickly, 'It wasn't your fault. You did your best.'

She took his hand and pulled him inside. More miserable than angry, she told him the whole story.

The the two men who'd called for Renata had been polite but firm. Ma had protested that Renata was a visitor. But once the men had checked her identity, they'd insisted she go with them.

'At least tell us where you're taking her,' Da had appealed, but the Guard said, not unkindly: 'Well, she is here illegally. But don't worry, she'll be all right.'

Da, distressed, had handed over her small case.

'We'll look after the sewing machine for you,' Ma told her. 'Maybe we'll be able to send it on.' But could Renata use it, wherever she was going?

Everyone had embraced her, Hetty whispering, 'Try and let us know where you are.'

And then she was gone.

Hetty and Ben were both silent, Renata's hopes dashed, and theirs too.

As the family started to appear for breakfast, no one said much. Even Solly – and even Mabel – were quiet. Ben had to leave. He'd promised Granny to go with her to early Mass to give thanks for Paddy's return. If only he could have given thanks for Renata too.

Very late the previous might, after Renata had been taken away, Hetty, sitting up in bed had groaned, 'Another hour and she would have been safe.'

Mabel, too dispirited to curl her hair, crawled into bed beside her. 'She's only a bit older than me. I thought we'd be friends. And she's got such a sad story.'

'I'd like to know how they found out she was here,' said Hetty, frowning.

'Well, Ben's family hadn't a chance to tell anyone,' said

Mabel. She yawned. 'Renata did say at supper that she thought a Guard might have spotted her making her way to Martin Street.'

Through the window the moon was a silver disc in the dark sky. As the clock ticked on the mantelpiece and Mabel began to snore, Hetty noticed in the pale moonlight that the painted girl had emerged from the weather house. Tomorrow would be fine. But where would Renata be, and when would they see her again?

* * *

Sunday passed in a kind of blur in both households. Hetty had to go her Hebrew class and then do her homework and help with the chores.

After Mass, though Granny and even Da had tried to cheer him up, Ben moped for the day, devastated that his hard-won plan had failed and wondering what on earth was happening to Renata now. Sean and Smiler couldn't even get him out for a football game.

Hetty was desperate to think of some way of finding Renata, and stormed around the house on her return from school, trying desperately to come up with a plan. But there was nothing she could do. Finally, Ma told her to take Solly for a long walk and to please keep out of the way for the whole afternoon.

25

Following Orders?

The sound of the milkman's horse clip-clopping up the street woke Ben the following morning. Sean heaved over, pulling the shrunken blanket off Ben and jerking him fully awake. Ben got out of bed and noiselessly pulled back the curtain. Below in the street the unmistakable figure of Renata, alone, suitcase in hand, was stepping into the Goldens' house!

Pulling on his clothes, Ben sped silently downstairs. He could hear the first birds singing in the trees beside the canal, and in the east the sky above the rooftops was streaked with pink. As he followed Renata inside, Hetty, an old coat over her pyjamas, held the door open for him with a welcoming smile.

The whole household was awake. Renata, exhausted and footsore, was back in the armchair, with Solly on her lap and Mossy barking a welcome. Ma and Mabel were making tea on the glimmer, though no one was watching out for the glimmer man. Every face was beaming, especially Renata's.

'What happened?' asked Ben urgently.

'I do not believe!' Renata's eyes shone. 'It is for me a miracle.' Ben, mystified, looked at Hetty. She laughed at him, her blue eyes bright, and offered him a hunk of bread.

Gradually the facts emerged. Renata was escorted first to the Garda Station, as they told her there was no train till early Monday morning. They had been quite nice to her, given her a sandwich, but no information. Because of her fear and worry, she'd got little sleep.

The next morning the immigration officer had come back for her, but when they got to Amiens Street Station very early on Monday morning the Guard had departed, leaving the immigration officer to deal with the situation alone.

'The Guard was nice,' said Renata. 'He carry my case. He wish me good luck.'

'But the immigration officer?' asked Mabel, bringing in the tea, while Hetty rushed to the kitchen to get bread and milk for Solly, and dump a bone from yesterday's soup into Mossy's tin dish, all at top speed for fear of missing anything.

'He look cross, and hold my arm while he buy ticket and bring me to platform.' She sniffed, and said to them all, half-laughing and half-sobbing, 'Where is Zaida with his, how you say, hanky?' Da smiled and handed her his own white linen handkerchief which Hetty recognised as one she'd embroidered with his initial, L, for his last birthday.

'Poor child, she's exhausted,' murmured Ma.

'But now I happy, too,' said Renata, burying her face in the hanky.

'But what happened then?' prompted Hetty.

Renata told them the officer was 'tall man in raincoat, with spectacles like Ben' – and she grinned across at him as he sat perched on a stool, listening.

She and the officer had sat on the bench in the chilly station to wait for the train.

'I am weeping, I cannot help ...' She sniffed again. 'The man say nothing but I know he is, how you say, not comfort?'

'Uncomfortable,' put in Ma.

I ask him, 'Where you taking me?'

The man had answered awkwardly that he could not say; that she did not have a valid residence permit and the law said she had to be deported.

'Back to Germany?' she had asked, horrified. 'Don't you know what happen there, to Jews?'

He told her uncomfortably that his orders were to put her on the Belfast train. The authorities there would decide whether she could stay or be sent to England. After a moment, he added quietly that she could be classified as an 'enemy alien' and might be interned. He lowered his head, unable to meet her eyes.

Renata tried to describe how a wave of anger had shot through her. 'Enemy?' she told him. 'I *not* enemy to Britain!

I on same side. Coming to Ireland save me. The *Nazis* are my enemy and Britain enemy, and enemy of all good people. They destroy my family, they take everything, they send Jews to terrible camps, they kill us–' She broke off, flooded with emotion.

The man glanced around anxiously, though there was no one else on the platform. He repeated very quietly, 'I have orders to put you on the train. But,' and he looked at her meaningfully, 'I've no way of knowing where you get off.' As he handed her the ticket he continued, 'Sure, you might even get off at the next station!' Renata waited, not sure if she understood.

Then he rose, saying he had to leave. 'D'you under-stand, Miss? Everyone will assume you're on the Belfast train.'

Only then did she realise that though she was still an illegal immigrant in Ireland, if she got off the train – or never actually got on it – no one would be looking for her.

'He say he has daughter at home of my age,' Renata told them, 'and he think it shame I cannot be safe with my family like her. He left, and I did not go on train. I come here.'

Amid the exclamations, Da said, 'In spite of this government, there are indeed many decent people in Ireland.'

* * *

Renata was too excited to sleep. Ma said gaily, 'Let's ask everyone to come for an early breakfast. Mrs O'Kelly from across the road brought in a gift of new-laid eggs from her hens yesterday, and we've some bread to toast ...'

'A breakfast party?' queried Da dubiously. 'On Monday morning?'

'Yes, a breakfast party to celebráte Renata's rescue!' cried Hetty. 'We'll make sure it's over in time for school and work.'

Da frowned. 'We should all keep a low profile. After all, she's still illegal here.'

'We'll tell them to slip in very quietly,' said Hetty. 'It's so early, hardly anyone's about yet.' Crackling with energy, she snapped out directions like an army general. 'Mabel, you go and get Bobba and Zaida–'

'It's too early to drag Bobba out, with her rheumatism,' protested Da.

'And Ben can get his Uncle Matt.'

'And Granny?' asked Ben. Granny was always up early.

'Of course,' Hetty agreed, 'everyone that helped. I'll go round to Eddie's, and we'll meet back here.'

Renata jumped to her feet. 'And *I* help with breakfast,' she said. 'I make scrambly egg!' They grinned as she followed Ma into the kitchen, leaving Da in his dressing gown, about to creep upstairs for a snooze.

But Ma put her head back around the kitchen door. 'Leon,' she said, smiling sweetly, 'as a special treat you can give the baby his early bottle.' He stopped in mid-step, sighed, and descended to scoop Solly into his arms complete with his toy rabbit, grabbing the bottle from Ma.

* * *

Ben rushed first to tell Granny the good news of Renata's return. She declared jubilantly that she would be thanking St Jude, patron saint of lost causes. Then he hurried around to Uncle Matt, who got dressed immediately, and, leaving Auntie Bridie and Paddy still asleep, returned with Ben to Number 19 to collect Granny.

Ben's Dad was already up, and Granny had told him the news. Then Mabel, who'd just brought Zaida into the Goldens', tapped on the open door.

'Er, my Ma sent me,' she said hesitantly when Ben invited her in. 'She asked … if your dad and Sean would like to come as well, she said it's a kind of party, and you're neighbours and …' Her voice faded away uncertainly.

Dad was taken by surprise. 'Well,' he said after a moment, 'it's good that the girl's … er … all right.' After a pause, he continued, 'But it's a bit early for me and I've to go to work–'

In a steely tone that they rarely heard, Granny said,

'Stephen, it's an invitation from a neighbour to a celebration – just for a cup of tea.'

All eyes were on him. 'Er, well maybe,' he said, embarrassed, glancing at Uncle Matt, 'I might drop in for a minute … before I leave for work … maybe I'll follow ye, when Sean's up …'

Ben was sure he wouldn't, but at least he'd been polite.

* * *

In a short time the crowd, jammed into the small parlour of the house in Martin Street, could scarcely move, and plates of scrambled egg were being handed around over people's heads.

Uncle Matt greeted the Goldens and said to Renata, 'You're welcome in our house as long as you like.' He patted her shoulder kindly. 'Our Paddy will be glad of the company. And I'll make enquiries through the union to try and track down your da – if he's still in Longford, it shouldn't be too hard.'

Renata threw her arms around him and kissed him on both cheeks. 'That is very kind,' she exclaimed. 'We say in German, *wunderbar*!' Uncle Matt, looking bashful, reached for his pipe.

Ben squeezed through the crowd to Zaida, sitting slightly bewildered in the armchair with his old greatcoat over his pyjamas. Amidst the commotion, he questioned

Ben about what had happened. As Mabel handed him a cup of tea he said slowly, 'We all prayed for this. But,' he added, 'we mustn't forget all the others in Europe, like Renata's family, who found no haven in Ireland or any-where else.' He gazed up at the photograph. 'Even at a good time like this, I think of whoever is left of my family in our little *shtetl*, at the mercy of the Nazis.' Then, forcing a smile, he touched Ben's shoulder. 'But we mustn't be sad; this is a happy day.'

A little later, Ben, threading his way to the kitchen in search of Hetty, noticed the front door open a crack and two figures squeeze into the packed room – his dad and Sean, both looking distinctly uncomfortable. Mrs Golden spotted them as she handed out plates, and gave her hus-band a look. He wriggled through the crowd and mut-tered nervously, 'You're both welcome.'

At the same moment Uncle Sam banged his spoon on a cup to capture attention. Hetty, coming down the stairs with Solly, who'd been woken up by the noise and wanted to join the party, rolled her eyes. Surely not some long speech, boring everyone and silencing the joy they all felt.

But Uncle Sam's speech was very short. 'This is a miracle – but it's also due to the determination of Hetty, Eddie, Ben and their families, and the good will of others whose names we don't even know. They all helped a brave young girl, our dear Renata, to escape from the

Nazi terror. We thank the Almighty.'

Hetty's da quickly added, 'Please, no one should say anything about Renata to anyone, she's still not out of danger.' He smiled, and, raising his teacup, proposed the age-old Jewish toast, '*L'Chaim*, to life!', echoed by most in the room.

Then Ben watched, amazed, as his own dad raised his cup and called, '*Sláinte*, good health.' As they all repeated it, he added gruffly, 'Sure, if I'd known there was a toast, I'd have brought in a *real* drink.' There was a burst of laughter, and Hetty's da said doubtfully, 'Our whiskey's run out and I don't think there's enough Kiddush wine–' But Uncle Matt called out, 'Wait, *I* happen to have a real drink with me,' and he produced from his coat pocket a half-bottle of his precious Irish whiskey.

'Ye have to go to work yet!' warned Granny.

'Ah sure, there's only enough for about two drops each – and it's just this once,' muttered Ben's dad as they passed it around to the adults.

Then Renata stood up on a chair and called out, blushing, 'I have only one word – *Danke schön* – thank you.'

Hetty, holding Mossy close, put in mischievously, 'That's two words, Renata.'

'Oh, trust you, Hetty,' said Mabel, and across the talk and laughter, Ben's eyes met Hetty's, erasing the distance between them.

* * *

Ben's dad, in rare good humour, put his hand on Ben's shoulder. 'Grand breakfast,' he said, 'but where were the rashers?'

Eddie, overhearing, grinned. 'None of those in a Jewish house, I'm afraid,' he murmured, 'but I bet you don't have cholent or kichels or matza!'

Shaking his head in puzzlement, Ben's dad said good-bye and brief thanks to the Goldens. As they left, Sean muttered to Ben, 'That Renata, she's a right little cracker!' Ben frowned, just like Hetty.

When they'd gone, Ben went into the kitchen, where Ma and Mabel were making a fresh pot of tea for Granny. His heart was so full that he gave Granny a hug, contentedly sniffing her familiar smell of peppermint and mothballs and lavender.

She said quietly, 'You see, Ben, God is good.' But as always, he knew she was thinking of his mam, and wishing, like him, that she too was part of this strange gathering.

But who knew, Ben thought – perhaps she wasn't far away, still watching over them?

26

The Reunion

It was nearly the end of the summer holidays, and in Martin Street a football game was again in full swing. Ben, who'd finally delegated a younger boy from two doors down to watch for the glimmer man, was in the thick of it. When a goal was scored, leaving Joey Woolfson, the goalkeeper, lying prone on the ground, there were cheers and groans.

Then the door of Number 17 flew open and Hetty, in a pink floral summer dress made by her Ma, which she hated, rushed into the street waving an envelope. 'Ben, quick, a letter from Renata!'

His open-necked Aertex shirt sticking to him in the heat, Ben was beside her in an instant. Examining the envelope with Hetty's address printed on it, he noted the stamps from the Sword of Light set, which Smiler was collecting. They'd keep it for him.

'Let's go to Eddie's and open it there!' And together they sped round to Donore Terrace.

* * *

Renata had stayed in Uncle Matt's for three weeks, often visiting the Goldens to help with sewing and to see

Mabel, Eddie and Hetty – and especially Solly – and the Byrnes, where Dad appeared to be slowly, awkwardly, getting used to her. She became a favourite with Granny who tried to explain Irish expressions to her: 'youngfella', 'oul' one' and 'scarlet', while Renata attempted the equivalent in German. And Sean, smitten with Renata, rushed home early to see her, and then was tongue-tied – unheard of for Sean – which amused them all.

Everyone now closely followed the worrying war news. The Nazis, in control of most of Europe, were advancing into Russia and Lithuania, and they were all aware that neither Zaida nor Renata had news of their families.

As time passed it had become increasingly difficult to keep Renata's presence secret, though no one, not even Ben's Dad, appeared to have let drop that she was a refugee. Some Martin Street residents, Jewish and Christian, such as Carmel and Maureen's family with whom Renata had become friends, must have suspected, yet she was accepted as a visiting foreign friend, and, as Uncle Matt put it, 'a grand young one'.

Uncle Matt, through fellow trade union members in County Longford, had soon tracked down Renata's father at Hirsch's Ribbons. 'Ireland's a small place,' he told Renata when he came in as she was having tea with Auntie Bridie and Paddy, and handed her a piece of paper with her father's address, watching joy light up her face.

Paddy, who was now off his crutches and keen to get back to the war, said, disappointed, 'You mean you won't be here for my next leave?'

* * *

Her departure had been marked by farewells, hugs and promises to keep in touch. 'Where is Zaida's hanky?' she'd sobbed. There were kisses for everyone on both cheeks, which rendered Sean speechless.

Hetty's Ma made sandwiches for the journey and a milky cake for her father. Uncle Sam gave her a ten shilling note from the family; Granny gave her a pair of scarlet wool gloves she'd knitted; and even Ben's dad said gruffly, 'Er, good luck now.' Zaida and Bobba presented her with two half-crowns and a packet of three large, white linen handkerchiefs. Zaida said gently, 'I hope you will not need them now for tears.'

But later when Ben and Hetty helped Renata carry her baggage and sewing machine to the station and waved her off, she leaned out the window, mopping her tears with one of the new hankies.

'Good thing my dad wasn't here,' Ben grinned to Hetty afterwards. 'Those kisses might've been a step too far!' He'd rather liked them himself, and although no one in

Ireland ever kissed anyone on both cheeks, he wondered, hopefully, if Hetty ever might. 'Still,' he went on, 'Dad's in better humour about things than he used to be.'

But Hetty wasn't thinking of his dad. She grabbed Ben's hand and, excitement in her eyes, said: 'We did it, Ben! We rescued her!' They had both laughed, happy it had all worked out.

* * *

When Ben and Hetty arrived with the letter, Eddie was in the front garden wearily helping his da pull up carrots and potatoes and load them into a wheelbarrow.

'Come to help?' asked Eddie hopefully. When they produced the letter, he hurried them into the kitchen, where Hetty opened it.

'Liebe Hetty, Ben, Eddie and everyone!'

You will be surprised at this letter – Papa is correcting it and his English is now very good!

The journey to Longford was six hours! The carriage was hot and we stopped many times. They told us there is little coal because of the Emergency – I think they mean the war, so they use for the engine, turf.

In our carriage we chatted, but you can be sure I said

nothing about myself, though one lady asked many questions.

There was a nun who I think guessed something – she gave me rosary beads and said she would pray for me.

Then, I got off at Longford very weary – and there on the platform was my dearest Papa, who I had not seen for so long. He wore his good grey suit and trilby hat that I remembered from Berlin. We were laughing and crying and I had to use again Zaida's hanky!

Papa's landlady has a small room which Papa asked to rent for me, though he does not earn much. She was not sure – until she saw my sewing machine! Now I do work for her instead of rent. More sewing! I wish Ma and Mabel were here to help.

It is good to be together, but underneath we are sad because there is no news of Mutti and Ella, or of Walter. Papa is still trying to contact them. He's certain one day our family will be together again. It is good Zaida and Granny and your families and the nun on the train, are all praying for us.

So for now, 'auf wiedersehen!' This means 'till we meet again'. I hope you will visit us here. I miss you all, and I feel now I have an Irish second family!

My love and thanks to all of you – mit ganzen Herz,

Renata

There was a silence after Hetty finished reading. 'I hope we see her again soon.' Her voice trembled.

'Come on, Hetty,' consoled Eddie. 'At least she found her father.'

'But her family in Warsaw ...' Hetty flared up, 'and all the terrible things that must be happening while we're safe here. I can't bear it!'

There was a tap on the window and Eddie opened the door for Zaida.

Greeting them, he noticed Hetty's emotion and gently pinched her cheek.

'Hetty, we'll have to find someone else for you to rescue,' he teased. Then, more seriously, 'My dear children, I know these are hard times, not only for Jews.' He glanced at Ben and they remembered his mam, and Paddy. 'We can weep a little, but we must march on like soldiers in a just war, and do the best we can. And,' he smiled round at them, 'that is what you all did.'

He added quietly, 'Like the rabbi said, "If I am for myself alone, what am I?"' And Ben recalled his mam's words in his autograph book, which he'd shown Hetty, 'Never send to know for whom the bell tolls' and thought, it says the same, really.

Zaida sank down in an armchair. 'Now, what about a drop of lemonade for an old man?'

Hetty, her spirits lifted by Zaida's words, told them,

'My friend Gertie's coming over. She wants us to go to Sandymount strand on the tram and bring sandwiches for a picnic.'

Ben asked quickly, 'Er ... can I come? And Smiler?'

'And me,' said Eddie.

'Well, if we're having an outing, Mabel will be home soon, she could do with cheering up,' Hetty said, with a sudden flash of kindness towards her sister.

Pleased to see Hetty back in her positive, organising mood, Ben put in, 'Maybe she'd like Carmel and Maureen to come too. We could all go!'

Zaida smiled, 'Go in good health.'

'We'll all meet at Number 17,' announced Hetty.

An hour later, laden with sandwiches, kichels, jam tarts, apples and lemonade, and tram fare scrounged from parents and relations, and with the two dogs racing around them, they all set off for the tram. By this time the numbers had grown to include more children from Martin Street who'd heard of the outing. At the last minute, Sean had arrived home on his bike, thrown it into the hall, and joined them, along with Billy and the Woolfsons.

Granny, Zaida and Hetty's ma, with Solly in her arms, waved them off, until the crowd turned the corner and were out of sight.

Then the adults heaved a sigh, and went into Number 17 to have a cup of tea.

Epilogue

Extracts from Renata's Diary 1941
Translated from the German

Longford, Ireland: September 1941

Papa and I waved goodbye to Hetty, Ben and Eddie, who visited us just before school began. It was *wunderbar* (they all understand that word now!) to see my good friends again. Hetty, so brave and strong, Ben, gentle but brave too, and Eddie to make us laugh. They brought good wishes from Mabel and the family – even Sean, who used to visit me in Dublin and sit blushing, never saying a word!

They all agreed my English is much better – but I still write my diary in German! Hetty told us that when she grows up she wants to be a journalist so she can make sure people know what's happening in other places and try to help.

Since they left, life is very quiet. Some people here are suspicious of us, but most are kind. I earn a little money from sewing. So far I haven't made any clothes for myself. The landlady, who is friendly now, enrolled me in a night class 'to improve my skills'. It is good we are safe here, but our family and my friends are in my mind. Now, at last, we received two letters. The news is good and it is bad ...

First the good: Dr Lowy's nephew, who emigrated to Palestine before the war, at last tracked Walter down and gave him our address. Last week a letter came with many stamps and postmarks!

Walter wrote that his ship, named by the passengers *The Promised Land* to remind them where they were going, was an old, leaky vessel, one of many that sailed to Haifa port laden with Jewish refugees from the Nazis. At least one sank on the way and all were drowned. Some ships were turned back by the British. But our brave Walter, though sick and very thin, he tells us, reached the 'Promised Land'.

He was sent first to a British detention camp in Atlit. 'It was not too bad,' he writes. 'I made friends there and learned Hebrew.'

After three months he was released and now lives on a kibbutz. 'Everyone, boys and girls, men and women, work together on the land, and study or play music in the evenings,' he says. 'We now grow enough to feed ourselves, and everything is shared.'

On the back of the letter was a drawing of Walter and a girl, both wearing shorts, picking oranges in an orchard. 'Making the desert bloom is hard work,' he writes, 'but at least we can hold our heads up and no longer live in fear of the Nazis.' He thinks the whole family is safely in Ireland, and says we'll all meet after the war ends.

Papa is happy that Walter is alive and well. I am too, but I wish I could hug my big brother again, and we could all be together like before.

Longford, Ireland: October 1941

I could not write the bad news last week, but here it is now. Because Papa could not get visas for Mutti and Ella – though he explained to the authorities that we would support ourselves – they are trapped by the war in Warsaw with the rest of Papa's family.

Papa wrote to the Red Cross, which helps families divided by the war to keep in touch. We had no reply until last week. The envelope was stamped by the International Red Cross, and on it was printed: HERR STERN, LANG FORD, IRLAND.

'Clever postman, to find us,' whispered Papa as he opened it with shaking hands. Inside was a letter in elegant Polish script, from his friend Casimir Pavlak who'd helped Mutti, Ella and me when we arrived from Berlin. As young men, Papa told us, they used to go fishing together in the river Vistula.

Papa frowned with concentration as he translated.

Dear friend Adam, I hope you and your daughter are settled in Irland. We are lucky we can send this special letter through the International Red Cross, where my daughter works. Since the war started, post is difficult, even to neutral countries.

Last year the Germans decreed all Jewish residents of Warsaw must move into the ghetto, sealed off by a wall over ten feet high, with barbed wire, guarded with dogs. We brought food for your dear wife, Janina, and for Ella, but we were turned back. There is fear and misery in the whole city, but it is worse in the ghetto. There are six or seven people to each room, and little food. There are rumours that trainloads of Jews from there are being taken to a concentration camp.

A few days ago we heard a tap at the door, and found Ella, thin and in rags. Though she is ten, you would take her for much younger. Despite the dangers, children slip in and out of the ghetto to smuggle in food, and also arms and ammunition, from Polish partisans. Ella says young people in the ghetto are determined to rise up and fight the Nazis, though I'm afraid they haven't much chance.

Ella brought a note from her mother, asking us to hide her until you could get her to Irland. Janina is not well. She writes: 'My husband's family are all here – the grandparents and the children suffer most. I will try to survive, though death is all around us. I hope Ella will have a better chance with you.'

Janina sent her deep love to you and Renata, and Walter, who she hopes is safe in Palestine. Ella told us Mutti will try to come for her one day, but she knows her dear Papa will find his little girl, even if it's not till the war is over.

Dear comrade, be sure we will care for Ella like our own child, and with God's help we will try to protect her from the Nazis. We pray Janina and the others too will survive this and your family can be reunited.

Your loving friends, Casimir and Berta.

PS Ella was not sure of your address and we hope you receive this.

Longford, December 1941

I haven't written my diary for a while. My heart has been heavy. Nothing is certain – the Pavlaks' letter gave us hope for Ella but fear for Mutti and for Papa's family.

Papa says we must be thankful that we ourselves, Walter and hopefully Ella have escaped the Nazis. 'Mutti is strong,' he told me gently, 'and there can be miracles. We must keep going, always with hope.' He's right, but inside I'm always fearful about my mother and my poor little sister.

Then a letter came from Hetty inviting us to visit them on the last day of Hanukkah. She said we will light the eight candles, and see all the family and our friends and neighbours in Martin Street. But she said they fear for Zaida's family.

The next day, Dr Lowy hurried in, waving a newspaper with huge headlines: 'PEARL HARBOUR BOMBED BY JAPAN: US AT WAR WITH JAPAN AND NAZI GERMANY.'

The landlady came upstairs. 'What does it mean?' she asked us. 'Why is everyone so excited?'

'It means, thankfully,' said Dr Lowy, 'that with America's help – and Russia's – Britain and the Allies will win the war and the Nazis will be destroyed. But it may take years.'

This news filled us all with hope. First I got one of Zaida's hankies and, mopping my tears, I started to look through the oddments of material in my box for something to make myself a new dress. And then I wrote to Hetty to tell them our family news, and say that on Hanukkah, in Dublin, we will all share our joy, and our sadness, together.

HISTORICAL NOTE

Jewish Immigration to Ireland

The first Jews arrived from Spain and Portugal in the 1500s. The earliest synagogue was opened in Crane Lane, Dublin, in 1660, and a Jewish cemetery in Fairview, dating from the early 1700s, can still be visited.

However, most of the present community are descended from Eastern European Jews who arrived in Ireland in the late 1800s and early 1900s, fleeing persecution and economic hardship.

The community spread to Irish towns such as Cork, Waterford and Drogheda, reaching a high point of 3500 in the mid-1940s. After that the number diminished. The 2006 census showed around 1200 Jews in Dublin, with a handful in Cork. The community continues to decline gradually, with people moving to the UK, Israel, the US and Australia.

Before the Second World War, the Irish government permitted a few European Jews to set up factories if they gave local employment, such as Hirsch Ribbons in the story (another was a hat factory, Les Modes Modernes, in Galway).

But, generally, Jewish refugees applying for visas to Ireland found no welcome. In 1995 Taoiseach John Bruton apologised to the community for Ireland's refusal to allow in Jewish refugees trying desperately to escape the Nazi terror in Europe.

Martin Street and Portobello

The Artisans Dwellings project was set up in 1876 to alleviate the unsanitary housing conditions of the Dublin working class, living in inner-city tenements. The project included Martin Street and Kingsland Parade in Portobello.

Later, Jewish immigrants settled in the Portobello area, the network of narrow streets between the South Circular Road and the Grand Canal. Clanbrassil Street was the colourful, bustling hub of Jewish Dublin, its kosher shops attracting both Jewish and other customers, especially on Sunday mornings.

In *Jewish Dublin, Portraits of Life by the Liffey* distinguished musician Colman Pearce describes the area:

My parents, born in 1913 and 1914 respectively, were both raised in that area off the South Circular Road affectionately known as 'Little Jerusalem' …

My mother often said, 'the best Christians among our neighbours are Jews!' This was meant as a sincere compliment, as she found much kindness and empathy with our Jewish neighbours. I was regularly asked by the orthodox Jewish families to perform minor tasks on the Sabbath – turning lights or gas on or off etc. We delighted to do this, as the rewards were always interesting (money!) or tasty (sweets, home-made fudge or – our favourite – matza crackers). We always considered ourselves fortunate to perform these little tasks in homes that were basically the same as our own, but also, mysteriously, magically and intriguingly different – and a little exotic.

The Main Characters

In researching this book, the author conducted numerous detailed interviews with current and former residents of 'Little Jerusalem', both Jewish and Christian. Many of the characters – including some of the Golden and the Byrne families – and events in the story are partly based on their recollections and partly fictional. (Names and some historical dates have been altered for the purpose of the story.)

Those based on fact include:

Zaida (Abel Golden), who left his *shtetl* (village) in the Russian empire, aged about seventeen. Like many refugees, he never knew his actual birthday.

As described in the story, he had only his father's coat, very little money and no identity papers. Over two years he walked and hitched across Europe, and, with the help of local Jews, worked at tailoring and farming along the way to feed himself.

Finally, in 1920-21, he reached Leeds in the north of England, meeting, for the first time, his eldest sister Mary (originally Mariashe), who had emigrated from home before he was born.

Abel and his wife, a Polish immigrant herself, later settled in Dublin and had two children, seven grandchildren and numerous great-grandchildren. Zaida and Bobba (Yiddish for Granny and Grandad) both died at a great age, but sadly, after the Germans invaded Poland, and later Russia and Lithuania, all the family members left behind were murdered in the Holocaust.

Zaida is still remembered by his family for his gentle jokes, his religious faith, and his lack of bitterness, despite poverty and persecution in his old home, then hardship as a new immigrant in a strange land. Living in Dublin, Zaida worked as a tailor, and made friends from all faiths, often meeting them in Bewley's Oriental Café in Grafton Street for tea and a chat.

Renata

Renata Stern is loosely based on a former German-Jewish refugee, who recounted her story to this author and others, in newspaper interviews and in Mary Rose Doorley's book, *Hidden Memories*.

Some of her family members are partly fictional, but the extraordinary circumstances of Renata's escape to Ireland with her father's help, and the humanity – in the end – of certain Irish individuals who allowed her to stay in the country, are based on her own account, and historically accurate.

She later married a British Jewish immigrant, had two sons, and lived in Dublin until her death a few years ago.

Uncle Matt and Granny

These characters grew from interviewees' recollections, memoirs and oral histories.

Matt: all the details of Uncle Matt – his clay pipe, his beloved birds and his forthright political attitudes and support of the trade union movement – are accurate.

Granny: based on an interview by the author with a Dublin woman who described the hardships of her Granny's childhood, and how her gentle, loving manner disguised her inner strength and resilience. Despite her troubles and her losses, she battled on, sustained by her spirit and her faith.

Stephen Byrne

He is also drawn from interviews, recollections and oral histories. There were certainly some who resented the 'foreigners' in their midst, and whose attitudes were similar to Stephen Byrne's. An incident resembling that of the returned cake is described in Ena May's book, *A Close Shave with the Devil: Stories of Dublin* (although in the original the gift is a hand-knitted baby dress).

In 1930s and 1940s Ireland, several anti-Semitic groups and organisations flourished, such as Maria Duce, the Blueshirts and also Sinn Féin – anti-Semitic articles appeared frequently in their newspaper, *An Phoblacht*, often written by Arthur Griffith.

However, it seems that in 'Little Jerusalem', with a few exceptions, relationships with neighbours across the religious divide were cordial, as described in Colman Pearce's memoir, and often led to warm and long-lasting friendships.

Jewish Religion and Festivals

Two Jewish festivals are referred to in the book: Passover occurs in spring, usually close to Easter, and Hanukkah in winter.

Passover

This commemorates the rescue of the Jewish people from slavery in Egypt, and their eventual settlement in the 'Promised Land'. The Seder is the traditional Passover meal at which wine is drunk and symbolic foods eaten, including matza (unleavened bread), reminding celebrants that their bread did not rise due to the haste with which, with divine intervention, they fled Egypt. (The Last Supper is thought to have been this Passover meal.) The story of the Exodus is re-told every Passover to educate the young, and remind all present of Jewish redemption and re-birth as a free people.

Hanukkah

This celebrates the miracle by which, as Hetty learns in her Hebrew class, the special holy oil used in the ancient Temple of Jerusalem, only sufficient for one day, actually lasted for eight days. During the eight-day festival, a special Hanukkah Menorah is lit. It has eight branches in a row, each topped by a candle-holder, and a holder for a special candle to light the others. It should be placed at a front window for all to see.

Jewish children were often given 'Hanukkah geld' (money), similar to First Communion money, or Hannukah gifts.

Sabbath

The weekly day of rest, from sunset on Friday to sunset on Saturday, is based on the Biblical commandment: 'Remember the Sabbath day to keep it holy.' This concept of a weekly day of rest, devotion and reflection – for all Jews, their servants and followers, even their work animals – was the origin of the modern weekend.

Orthodox Jews are required to abstain from work of all kind – even, as in the story, lighting a fire or switching on a lamp, and to join the congregation in prayer in the synagogue.

Barmitzvah

Coming up to the age of thirteen, a Jewish boy studies the rules and history of his religion. In the synagogue, usually on the Sabbath, he recites part of the weekly 'portion of the holy law' (the Torah) inscribed on a parchment scroll, and he undertakes the responsibilities of a Jewish man.

In more recent times, twelve-year-old orthodox girls also follow a course of study, culminating in a group ceremony known as Bat Chayil. However, in Progressive congregations, of which there is one in Dublin, boys have a Barmitzvah and girls a Bat Mitzvah, for which they both study and perform the reading in the synagogue.

There is also – as seen in the story – rejoicing, with gifts, and parties for families and friends.

The Holocaust, or 'Shoah'

(Shoah is a biblical word meaning 'calamity')

Even before the war started, the planned destruction of the Jewish people by the German Nazi party began. In neutral Ireland, with press and radio censorship, very little was published about the Holocaust.

In the world press and on the BBC, there was some information about Nazi concentration and slave labour camps in Germany, and, later, those in Poland and in Nazi-occupied Europe.

But information was also spread by word of mouth and other means. From 1933 when the Nazi party took power, German newspapers and radio made clear that the Nazi policy was the destruction of all Jews. The camps of Buchenwald, Dachau and Sachsenhausen were set up in Germany well before the war began. 'Kristallnacht', the Night of Broken Glass, in November 1938, alerted Jews and others to the level of Nazi hatred and violence towards the Jews.

In September 1939 a British Government White Paper gave horrific details of the treatment of Jewish prisoners in Dachau.

When the camps were liberated by British, Russian, American and other Allied soldiers, the full horror of the deaths of millions in gas chambers, or from disease and starvation, or in mass shootings, was finally revealed.

Of those in the story, sadly, people like Mutti and all Renata's relations in the Warsaw ghetto would have been deported to their deaths.

There were many brave people, like the Pavlaks in the story, who, at great risk to themselves, kept children like Ella hidden until the end of the war.

German 'special' forces, the *Einsatzgruppen* who followed in the wake of the German army as it advanced first into Poland, and later Russia and Lithuania, would have rounded up and killed Zaida's family along with thousands of Jews living in the towns and *shtetls* of Eastern Europe.

It took a long time after the end of the Second World War in Europe in May 1945 for the relatives of victims of the Nazis to find out, with the help of the International Red Cross, what had happened to their loved ones in Europe. Some never did.

In all, six million Jews, including a million and a half children, were killed in the Shoah.

Wartime Bombings in Neutral Ireland

There were, of course, thousands killed in Nazi bombing raids on Britain and elsewhere. The Belfast Blitz on Easter Tuesday 1941 wrought huge destruction, killing almost 900 people and injuring another 1500 in a single night.

And, despite its neutrality, there were several bombing incidents in the South of Ireland, including attacks on Irish ships and on the mail boat, *The Cambria*.

In August 1940 three girls were killed by German bombs in County Wexford. In January 1941 bombs fell on Dublin, first on Terenure, then on the Dolphin's Barn area, as described in the book, destroying at least three houses, injuring twenty people and damaging the synagogue. However, the worst incident occurred on the night of 31 May 1941 when bombs were dropped first on the Phoenix Park (causing mayhem at the zoo and shattering all the windows of Áras an Uachtaráin), and also at Ballybough. Later that night four high-explosive bombs did major damage in the North Strand area, leaving 32 dead and over 80 injured.

The Warsaw Ghetto

After the German occupation of Poland in September 1939, which triggered the Second World War, Warsaw, Poland's capital, contained the largest ghetto in Europe; from November 1941 more than 400,000 Jews were imprisoned within its walls in unbelievable conditions of overcrowding, hunger and disease.

Although the ghetto was sealed, a few children, like Ella in the story, slipped in and out despite the risks, to smuggle in food, and later, arms.

By 1942, thousands of Jewish men, women and children had been deported by the Nazis from the ghetto, packed in cattle trucks, to Treblinka death camp. Many of those remaining were determined to resist their German oppressors. The Jewish Fighting

Organization, which included both men and women, issued a call: 'All are ready to die as human beings.' Secretly they fortified hide-outs and bunkers, obtaining some rifles and ammunition from Polish resistance leaders outside.

The Warsaw Ghetto Uprising began on 19 April 1943 – the second night of Passover – and continued until the ghetto was destroyed by bombing and artillery, virtually all its inhabitants killed or captured. The Nazis planned to liquidate the ghetto within three days, but the Jews bitterly resisted for twenty-seven days, longer than several European countries! Their chances of survival were minimal, but they chose to fight and die 'to defend the honour of the Jewish people'.

Trade Union Mass Demonstration

Although the date has been slightly altered for the purposes of the story, the Mass Demonstration against the anti-Trade Union Bill and the wage freeze took place in College Green before a huge crowd; James Larkin did, indeed, set fire to a copy of the Bill as described in the story.

Ben's mother Marie, an intelligent, self-educated woman from a political family, correctly mentions Michael Davitt and James Connolly as opponents of anti-Jewish prejudice.

TB (Tuberculosis)

Also known at the time as 'consumption', the illness is caused by organisms called *bacilli* attacking the lungs, forming cavities and eating their way into the bronchial tubes. The symptoms include loss of appetite, persistent, short staccato coughing, hoarse voice, and, in the later stages, coughing up blood.

TB thrived in poor social conditions, such as overcrowded tenements with minimal hygiene and poor diet. But the disease, rife in Ireland and Britain in the nineteenth and early twentieth centuries, also hit the well-off, and many of its victims were young or in their prime.

Frequently the disease was seen as a social stigma, to be discussed in lowered voices, and people avoided mentioning sick family members.

Various remedies were tried – travelling, when possible, to a warm, dry climate, rest, wholesome food, and fresh mountain air. Pine trees were thought to be helpful, which was why they were planted around Crooksling and other sanatoriums. Medical intervention, such as collapsing the lung by injecting air into it, were mostly ineffective.

When Dr Noel Browne became Irish Minister of Health in 1948, he built several sanatoriums like Crooksling, and is credited with greatly alleviating the disease in Ireland. Many of his own family had died from TB, and he explained that it was difficult for later generations to appreciate the sense of desolation and suffering associated with the disease, which afflicted one in ten families and wiped out whole communities. Noel Browne described the primitive fear, bred by ignorance, which caused passengers on a bus in the 1950s to hold their breaths when they came within half a mile of a sanatorium.

Despite Noel Browne's energy and determination, and even with help of funds from the Hospitals Sweepstake, it was not until the mid-1950s, with the discovery of streptomycin, that the disease was more or less conquered in Ireland.

However, new, resistant strains of the disease are still a major problem in parts of the world, such as Africa.

BIBLIOGRAPHY

Benson, Asher: *Jewish Dublin; Portraits of Life by the Liffey*, A&A Farmar, 2007

Conaghan, Michael, Ed: *The Grand Canal*, Office of Public Works, 1992

Corcoran, Michael: *Through Streets Broad & Narrow: a history of Dublin trams*, Midland Publishing, 2000

Crowley, Elaine: *Cowslips & Chainies: A Memoir of Dublin in the 1930s*, Lilliput Press, 1996

Daiken, Leslie: *Out Goes She; Dublin street rhymes*, Dolmen, 1963

Daiken, Leslie: *The Circular Road*, script of play broadcast on Radio Éireann 1959

Doorley, Mary Rose: *Hidden Memories*, Blackwater Press, 1994

Gray, Tony: *The Lost Years; the Emergency in Ireland 1939-1945*, Little Brown 1997

Johnston, Máirín: *Around the Banks of Pimlico*, Attic Press, 1985

Johnston, Máirín: *Dublin Belles: Conversations with Dublin Women*, Attic Press, 1988

Kearns, Kevin C: *Dublin Voices, an oral folk history*, Gill & Macmillan 1998

McCarron, Donal: *'Step Together!' Ireland's Emergency Army 1939*, Dublin, 1999

McGrath, Eamonn: *The Charnel House*, Blackstaff Press 1990

MacThomáis, Éamonn: *Me Jewel and Darlin' Dublin*, O'Brien Press, 1974

MacThomáis, Éamonn: *Gur Cakes & Coalblocks*, O'Brien Press, 1976

May, Ena: *A Close Shave with the Devil: Stories of Dublin* Lilliput Press, 1998

Nowlan, Kevin, Ed: *Ireland in the War Years & After.* Gill & Macmillan, 1969

O'Donnell, E. E., Ed: *Father Browne's Dublin: Photographs 1920-1950,* Wolfhound Press, 1993

O'Keeffe, Phil: *Down Cobbled Streets; a Liberties Childhood,* Brandon, 1995

Rice, Eoghan: *We are Rovers: an oral history of Shamrock Rovers,* Nonsuch Publishing, 2005

Rivlin, Ray: *Shalom Ireland; A Social History of Jews in Modern Ireland,* Gill & Macmillan, 2003

Read Marilyn Taylor's
other historical novel